"Why did you ask me out?"

Angel managed a smile. "I seem to remember you asking me out."

"You asked first."

"That's a technicality."

"But still the truth." Hunter didn't let go of her hand but lowered it so that it rested against his wet chest.

Was he trying to short-circuit her neglected libido?

"I guess I just saw you in a different light." A neon one that screamed, *Look at how sexy this man is!*

"It was the brownie, wasn't it?" he said, teasing. "The power of chocolate."

"Well, that didn't hurt." Should she tell him the truth? Would it sound shallow? "Although if you hadn't looked so good in those jeans up on the gallery roof, the brownie likely wouldn't have been enough by itself."

The grin that formed on his face could only be described as rakish, a look she didn't think he wore very often.

"That right?"

Dear Reader,

You have in your hands the story of the last of the five adopted Hartley siblings. Angel is the youngest, and I've been looking forward to telling her story for a long time. Her journey is one of not only finding a forever kind of love with a truly awesome man, but also one of discovering who she is in the literal sense. I also wanted to show that love and self-worth should not depend on the color of one's skin but rather on the kindness and compassion in one's heart. I chose to make Angel Native American because I have from my earliest memories had a great and inherent affection and respect for the Native peoples who first lived on this land that became America and who still protect their legacies and culture. They were the first victims of the racism we are still dealing with to this day. I hope in some small way to combat that racism with this story of love, acceptance and embracing one's heritage.

I can't begin to thank you all for the support, kindness, positive reviews and love you've given to my books, and especially the Blue Falls, Texas series, over the past decade. It truly means the world to me. For now, this is the last story from Blue Falls, but one never knows what the future might hold.

If you'd like to keep in touch and be alerted to when I have new books coming out, visit trishmilburn.com to sign up for my newsletter and to find links to my various social media accounts. I look forward to hearing from you.

Trish

HOME *on the* RANCH

TEXAS COWBOY, BE MINE

— ☙ —

TRISH MILBURN

H HARLEQUIN® HOME ON THE RANCH

Recycling programs
for this product may
not exist in your area.

ISBN-13: 978-1-335-50864-5

Home on the Ranch: Texas Cowboy, Be Mine

Copyright © 2018 by Trish Milburn

Printed in U.S.A.

Trish Milburn writes contemporary Western romance for Harlequin Books. She's a two-time Golden Heart® Award winner, a fan of walks in the woods and road trips, and a big geek girl, including being a dedicated Whovian and Browncoat. And from her earliest memories, she's been a fan of Westerns, be they historical or contemporary. There's nothing quite like a cowboy hero.

Books by Trish Milburn

Harlequin Western Romance

Blue Falls, Texas

Her Perfect Cowboy

Having the Cowboy's Baby

Marrying the Cowboy

The Doctor's Cowboy

Her Cowboy Groom

The Heart of a Cowboy

Home on the Ranch

A Rancher to Love

The Cowboy Takes a Wife

In the Rancher's Arms

The Rancher's Surprise Baby

Her Texas Rodeo Cowboy

Twins for the Rancher

Visit the Author Profile page
at Harlequin.com for more titles.

To the best editor a gal who dreamed of writing books could have ever asked for. I count myself beyond lucky to have worked with Johanna Raisanen from day one of my Harlequin career. Jo, you're not only a fantastic editor but an awesome friend—even if you are a Maple Leafs fan. Go, Predators! LOL!

Chapter 1

No, that still wasn't right. Angel Hartley took another couple of steps backward, wondering if a bit more distance would correct the crooked photo frame. She even closed her eyes for a few seconds before giving the large image of a bull rider sitting atop a fence another look. Nope, still crooked.

Before she could approach the wall, however, Merline Teague, owner of the art gallery, stepped into her path and held up her hand.

"The piece is fine how it is," Merline said.

"It's still crooked."

Merline shook her head. "No, you just think it is. I learned early on that the longer I stared at any art I'd hung—especially if it was my own—the more uneven I thought it was." She gestured around at several other works Angel had already placed on the walls. "Everything looks great so far."

"Are you sure?" Because Angel wanted the show featuring her hard work to be perfect, so perfect that people attending wouldn't be able to resist buying something to take home with them.

"Positive. Remember, it's in my best interest as well that your opening be a smashing success."

Well, that was true. Merline might be one of the nicest people Angel had ever met and this gallery a passion project, but it was also a business that needed to make money to stay open.

"Sorry. I might be obsessing a little."

Merline smiled and started to speak, but whatever she'd been about to say was drowned out by the sound of banging on the roof.

Angel looked up. "What in the world?"

"Forgot to tell you I was having some roof repairs done today since the gallery's closed. Had a bit of damage from the storm last week. Wanted to fix it before another storm could make it worse."

Made sense. Late spring in Texas was no stranger to violent weather.

Merline's phone rang and she moved toward her office as she answered the call. Angel made one final perusal of the photo in front of her before moving on to a smaller piece showcasing her family's cattle herd silhouetted against a gorgeous twilight sky. After hanging only two more of her works, however, she couldn't stand the banging anymore and decided to break early for lunch. Maybe whoever was up on the roof would be done when she returned.

After checking with Merline to see if she wanted anything and finding out the older woman had brought her lunch, Angel headed out the front door. Her phone dinged with a text, causing her to pause. She yelped and dropped her phone when something fell from the sky right in front of her.

Her heart was still hammering away when she realized it was a piece of lumber with bits of torn shingles attached to it. Not to mention some wicked-looking nails. And it hadn't fallen from the sky but rather had been pitched from the roof.

"Are you okay?"

Her hand pressed against her chest, she looked up but couldn't see the guy's face since he was backlit by the strong midday sun.

"Are you hurt?" As he moved quickly to the ladder, she recognized him. By the time she'd taken another breath, Hunter Millbrook was on the ground striding toward her.

"I'm fine," she finally managed to say. "Just scared the living daylights out of me."

"I'm so sorry," Hunter said as he took off his hat and ran his hand through his sandy-brown hair.

Angel got the impression that his heart might very well be galloping as fast as hers. Still...

"You may want to toss heavy objects somewhere other than over the front door."

"I had been," he said, nodding toward a pile of roofing detritus lying on the ground at the side of the building. "That one got away from me when I accidentally grabbed a nail." He held up his hand, which did indeed have a trickle of blood on the palm, as if she required proof of what he was saying.

"Ouch," she said with a wince. "You should wash that and apply some antibiotic cream so it doesn't get infected." She stopped short of asking if his tetanus vaccination was up-to-date.

Hunter stared at her with a confused expression on his face for a few seconds before a small smile tugged at the edge of his mouth.

An odd little flutter in her middle made Angel feel suddenly very awkward and at a loss for what to say or do.

"I almost hit you on the head with a two-by-four and you're concerned about a minor injury to me?"

She shrugged. "It's a mom thing. Six years of tending boo-boos."

The smile faded from Hunter's face, and Angel found she missed it immediately. Hunter looked inexplicably sad without it.

"Let me make it up to you," he said as he grabbed the offending two-by-four and heaved it onto the pile of debris. "How about lunch?"

That strange flutter reappeared as if a butterfly had just emerged from its cocoon and was trying out its wings. Was Hunter asking her out? If so, that was…unexpected. No, she was seeing intent that wasn't there.

"At least I hope a special at the Primrose will make up for my clumsiness."

She waved off his offer, perhaps with a bit too much gusto. "It's not necessary. I was just running out to take care of some errands."

Errands? No, she'd been going for lunch, the very thing he was offering. So why did she feel the overwhelming need to do anything but accept his kind offer? Hunter had never done anything to her. She really didn't even know him that well considering he'd been ahead of her in school by three years. He'd been in the graduating class the year she was a freshman, a gulf between their ages and classes that was not easy to cross. Not that she'd wanted to.

Back then she'd had a crush on Chris Ross, a mere sophomore. Of course, he hadn't noticed her any more than Hunter and his fellow seniors had. Well, not until her sophomore year anyway. They'd dated for a while until he'd proved what an ass he was and she'd berated herself for ever giving him a second thought, let alone the entire fall semester.

She'd dated off and on after that, but nothing had been serious until Dave. And that had worked out like water-soaked toast. Except for Julia. Her daughter was the love her life, and there was nothing she wouldn't do to protect her and make her happy. Admittedly it was often a struggle between being a good mother and being too indulgent because Julia's father had abandoned her.

Angel knew what it felt like to be abandoned by a parent. As if the person who was supposed to love you more than life itself either couldn't or wouldn't. In other words, like complete and utter garbage.

Realizing she'd gotten lost in her thoughts, heat rushed up her neck to her face. Thank goodness for her darker complexion. Her very fair and very blond sister, Sloane, would have no such cover in this type of situation. But Angel's unknown Native American background was a lifesaver sometimes.

"Well, I'll let you get back to work," she said. "Try not to jab any more nails into your hands."

The barest hint of a smile made a brief appearance on his face before he nodded and turned back toward the ladder. When she had to resist reaching out to him, saying something to alleviate what felt like his disappointment, she shook her head and turned toward her truck. Maybe all the banging on the roof had jarred something important loose in her brain because never before had she had such a reaction to someone she'd known since she was a kid.

She felt marginally better once she was in the confines of her vehicle with the air-conditioning blowing on her face full blast. But then she made the mistake of glancing back at the gallery right at the moment Hunter bent over to pick up a pry bar. It wasn't the first time she'd seen a man do incredible things for a pair of worn jeans, but Lord have mercy, Hunter could give all the rest a powerful run for their money.

Hunter's heart rate still wasn't back to normal when he looked over his shoulder as Angel Hartley left the parking lot, her truck spitting gravel. He couldn't help but think she probably was in a hurry to get far away from him. After all, he'd nearly caused her serious injury. The idea of that board, maybe even one of the twisted nails, hitting her in the head caused a cold chill to rush over him despite the intensity of the late May sun beating down on his back.

And of all the people that he could have almost injured, it had to be her. Ridiculous as it sounded even in his own head, he'd had a crush on that woman for close to a decade. He'd imagined dozens of different ways of asking her out, had even been on the verge once—and not the clumsy offer he'd just made to buy her lunch. But fate had this ugly habit of interfering, making him believe that it just wasn't meant to be.

He supposed he was lucky that he didn't see her that often and so he could go for long periods and not even think about her. Well, that wasn't exactly true. Whenever he thought about having a family of his own, it was always her face that he imagined as his wife. Which was crazy considering how few words they'd ever exchanged and how little time they'd spent anywhere near each other.

Either she'd been dating someone, or he had. Then his dad had died and Hunter was suddenly responsible for the ranch and his mom, for making ends meet however he could. Which was why he was on the roof of Merline Teague's art gallery, why he occasionally drove a load of cattle to market for other ranchers, why he didn't have time for a social life.

Then there was his mom…

Hot as a lit fuse on the end of a firecracker and with his stomach beginning to growl, he climbed back down the ladder and retrieved the cooler containing his lunch from his truck. He sat with his back against a large live oak tree and took a long, slow drink of water. After downing a few bites of his ham-and-cheese sandwich to quiet the growling in his middle, he pulled out his phone and called home. With each ring that went unanswered, he got more nervous. Was today the day his mom forgot something so important it could endanger her life?

"Hello." At the sound of his mom's voice, he breathed a sigh of relief.

"Hey, Mom. Just checking in while I eat my lunch."

"Doing fine, dear."

He heard the frustration in her voice, though she tried to hide it. For a woman who'd always worked hard, always stayed busy with half a dozen different projects to help others, the diagnosis of early-stage Alzheimer's disease had been a difficult one to take. At first she'd been in denial, maintaining that forgetting things was just a part of getting older. When she'd finally faced the truth, she'd alternated between angry and sadder than he'd seen her since the months after his dad died. In truth, his moods had followed the same pattern. It was so unfair that he first lost his father to a sudden heart attack, and now he was being forced to watch his mom slowly slip away.

He took a deep breath, reminding himself to focus on the positive. Today was one of her better days, almost as if the disease didn't lurk just under the surface. He could almost convince himself that when she'd not been able to locate the cocoa the night before, it was nothing more than any normal person misplacing something. Only the fact that the cocoa was where it always was indicated something more sinister was going on.

"Good. What are you up to today?"

"Been doing laundry." Which meant when he got home he'd have to make sure she'd remembered to put the wet clothes in the dryer so they didn't end up with sour clothing sitting in the washing machine again. "Mildred called a little while ago. She's going to come over and visit for a bit while the lawn guy is mowing at her place. She hates the noise."

In reality, Mildred was among the group of his mom's friends who had offered to check in on her when he had to be away from the ranch. They'd all done a good job of not letting his mom have any clue that they weren't merely visiting but rather making sure she was okay. He hated being sneaky, but he also knew his mom's pride had taken a lot of punishing blows because of her disease. If he could take years off his own life in order to free her from her diagnosis, he'd do it in a heartbeat.

"That's good. Tell her I said hello."

"Will do. You're staying out of this hot sun, aren't you?"

Hard to do when you were working on a roof. "I'm fine, Mom. You don't have to worry about me. Just enjoy your visit with Mildred."

After they chatted about a couple of inconsequential things, she said she had to go because Mildred was at the door. He finished eating his sandwich, then bit into one of the brownies his mom had made the night before. He waited for some terrible taste to make his tongue revolt like the time she'd put salt in his coffee, but he relaxed when his taste buds encountered only the familiar delicious chocolate. It was moments like this that he could almost believe his mom wasn't ill. If only that were true.

He leaned his head back against the tree, closed his eyes and tried to think about anything other than how every day brought him closer to losing his mother, at least the woman she'd always been. He couldn't think of a crueler fate than to lose one's mind.

The sounds of vehicle engines mixed with the rattle of a horse trailer passing by. In the distance, he heard the laughter of children. Must be coming from the elementary school, which wasn't far away.

Thoughts of school led his mind back to Angel. He remembered the first day he'd seen her his senior year. She was a freshman then and wore that wide-eyed and apprehensive look so many freshmen did every year. He knew he'd seen her before, likely in town with her family, but she'd looked different that day in the hallway as she worked the combination on her locker. She was becoming more of a woman, leaving the kid she'd been behind. Still, she'd seemed so young, and he was sort of dating a girl from nearby Poppy then. That had lasted all of three weeks, and he suspected it had just as much to do with his attraction to Angel as it had Sarah's decision that she just wasn't that into him.

For a while, he'd convinced himself Angel was too young to date, especially since she had four older siblings who'd no doubt have had his hide if he hurt her in any way, real or imagined. When he finally realized his attraction wasn't going away, word was she had the hots for Chris Ross. And in what seemed like the next moment, though it had in fact been the following year, she began dating him.

Chris's dad was the district attorney, and his mom had one of those home-based businesses where she sold stupidly expensive makeup. She must have done well, judging by the way she traded for a new, shinier, higher-priced car each year. How was he, the only son of ranchers who barely scraped by, supposed to compete with that? Not to mention that after she and Chris broke up, Hunter was still grieving the recent death of his father.

"Hon, you can come inside and enjoy your lunch in the air-conditioning."

Hunter jerked out of the past as if he'd been physically yanked by the sound of Merline's voice. He opened his eyes to see her standing a few feet away.

"I'm okay, thanks. Easier to go back up on the roof after sitting here than inside."

"Don't you get too hot up there. Can't have you suffering a heatstroke and tumbling off."

"I won't."

Though when the time came to climb back up the ladder, he could think of no less than five hundred things he'd rather be doing.

He looked inside the brown paper bag that had held his lunch, eyeing the second brownie that remained. As he stood, he folded the top of the bag over, then headed toward the entrance to the gallery. When he stepped inside, he heard Merline's voice coming from her office. Good, she was on the phone. He grabbed a black marker sitting atop the front counter and wrote Angel's name on the bag before leaving his chocolate peace offering for her.

As he turned to leave, he caught sight of a large framed photograph on a freestanding wall facing the entrance. It was a close-up of a steer wrestler with his arms wrapped around a steer's horns and his face set in determination. The informational tab below the print revealed Angel as the photographer, which would explain why she'd been in the gallery earlier. He was far from an art critic, but the photo was really good, capturing a moment so fast and so far removed from the normal human eye that no one could ever really see it. And yet Angel had caught it with a snap of her camera. Not only was she beautiful, she was also really talented.

"She does great work, doesn't she?"

Hunter had been so absorbed in admiring the photo that he hadn't heard Merline's approach for a second time. He better not allow himself to get that distracted while up on the roof.

"Yeah. I do well if I don't cut off people's heads in photos."

Merline laughed. "You should come to the exhibit opening."

"I stay pretty busy." Not to mention he'd stick out at an art exhibit opening like a hipster at a rodeo.

"How is your mom doing?" Merline asked, seeming

to guess the real reason he couldn't just go out and do whatever he wanted whenever the urge struck him.

"Good days and bad."

"It's a tough thing to deal with, but she's a strong woman. And you're a good son."

"Thank you."

"You should bring your mom. I bet she'd like it."

But what if she had one of her bigger lapses in memory? She'd hate for that to happen in public where everyone might stare at her. But maybe he'd ask her about it anyway. He honestly didn't think it was good for her to hide herself away on the ranch for fear of looking feeble of mind. He worried that it might actually cause the disease to progress faster. If he worded the idea in such a way that it seemed she was doing him a favor, maybe she'd agree.

Hunter left the building when Merline's phone rang again. He resisted the urge to grab the paper bag on the way out, fearing his gift was too cheesy.

After being inside, the exposure to the cooler air made it feel as if he was stepping through the gates of Hades when he climbed back up on the roof. But he couldn't put it off any longer. He needed to finish this job as quickly as he could so he could get paid and not have to depend on others to check up on his mom. He appreciated their kindness, but it didn't sit well with him not being the one there if she needed anything. After all, she'd been there for him every day of his life, not a series of babysitters.

Yes, logically, he knew he had to work. The bills, including those for his mom's doctor visits, wouldn't get paid if he didn't. And yet he still felt as if he should be the one there if his mom's memory abandoned her, if she forgot something crucial and endangered herself. He closed his eyes and tried to push away all the things he could worry about because it didn't do anyone any good to borrow trouble. Not his mom, not him, no one.

He'd been back to work about half an hour when the sound of a vehicle pulling into the lot drew his attention. A glance revealed it was Angel returning from her errands. Part of him wanted to tell her he liked her photograph, but common sense stepped up to the plate and reminded him that engaging with Angel any further would just make him wish for something he couldn't have. If he didn't have time to come out to a gallery opening, he sure didn't have time to go on a date. And chances were, after he'd almost knocked her on the head, she wouldn't be receptive to the idea of going out with him anyway.

That was probably for the best considering the demands on his time right now. But even knowing that, he couldn't shed the feeling of disappointment that came with the realization. Once he was fairly certain Angel had made it inside, he paused to wipe the sweat off his forehead and looked at the sparkling expanse of the lake in the distance. Several boats dotted the surface, people enjoying a day of freedom and relaxation. Sometimes when he thought about the sudden loss of his dad and the cruel diagnosis for his mom, it was enough to make him ponder the possibility of past lives, that maybe he hadn't been a good person in one of them and now was being punished as a result. The only problem was he wasn't the only one paying the price.

Chapter 2

Angel had done her best to not look up at Hunter as she'd walked toward the gallery, but it proved as impossible as resisting the last slice of her mom's scrumptious chocolate cake. She'd half expected to find him watching her when she lifted her gaze, but she was greeted by his back. Though that should have been a relief, she instead found herself disappointed. Honestly, it was as if she were the one up on that roof having her brain baked. Hunter wasn't interested in her. He'd just been concerned that he'd almost hit her. He would have reacted the same way if it had been Merline who'd nearly caught a two-by-four to the head.

And why in the world was she wondering if Hunter Millbrook found her attractive? Yes, he was a fine-looking man, but it wasn't as if she'd just realized that. That piece of information would fall under the heading of Common Knowledge. It was sort of surprising that he wasn't married yet. Maybe he was dating someone. After all, she wasn't like town matchmaker Verona Charles and in the know about everyone's love life.

She was overthinking the whole situation. After all, he hadn't even noticed her return. Maybe her mind was looking to obsess about something else so she wouldn't freak out over the possibility that her gallery opening might be a colossal failure like the one her sister, Sloane, had held. Granted, Sloane's exhibit had been paintings made by the ranch's horses and cows. But it had also been an attempt to make money for a good cause, Sloane's ranch camps for underprivileged kids. By contrast, Angel's was simply a career move.

Sure, she'd had some interest in her work and a few of her photos published in national publications, but it wasn't as if her work was Met-worthy. Still, it seemed to be where her heart and her talent had led her when she needed to help provide for her daughter. She knew her family would always be there to lend a hand, but Julia was her responsibility. And her daughter was never going to suffer because her father had abandoned her. If Angel had anything to say about it, Julia would know that everyone in her life loved and cherished her despite Dave's absence. Angel couldn't stand the idea that her daughter would ever be abandoned like Angel herself had been—twice.

Angel did her best to shake off the negative thoughts. She hated when she allowed herself to dwell on them too much, especially in light of the fact that she truly had a good life with a wonderful family who had chosen her. Who'd taken in a baby of a different race and never once acted as if it was anything other than completely awesome. There were a ton of people in the world who could learn basic human decency from her parents.

Realizing she'd been standing just inside the entrance to the gallery while her mind had gone spinning off in what seemed like every direction, she let out a breath and started forward. That was when she happened to look over at the front counter and saw a paper bag with her name written on it. Curious, she retrieved the bag and opened it to find a brownie inside along with a note that said simply, "Sorry again."

She looked upward, as if she could see Hunter through the ceiling. It was a nice gesture, and coming as it did right when she was craving chocolate, it made her smile.

"Well, you look to be in a better mood than you were earlier," Merline said as she came out of her office with a stack of brochures about the gallery to refill the holder on the front counter.

Angel wiggled the brownie. "Amazing how chocolate in hand can do that."

"From the bakery?"

"Nope." Angel pointed at the roof. "Hunter almost hit me in the head with lumber when I was leaving. I think this is a peace offering."

"Oh, I'm so glad you didn't get hurt. For your sake and his. That boy has too much to worry about already."

Angel kept quiet about how Hunter had ceased being a boy a long time ago and was definitely 100 percent man. Maybe he did seem like a kid to Merline considering she was a grandmother.

"Is the roof that bad?"

Merline shook her head. "Should be fine in a few days, but that wasn't what I was talking about. He's got that ranch to run by himself, too, and now his mom to care for."

"His mom? Is she sick?" Now that she thought about it, she hadn't seen Mrs. Millbrook around town in a while.

"Poor woman has early-stage Alzheimer's disease. Hunter says she has good days and bad."

"That's terrible."

It just proved what she already knew—life wasn't fair and bad things happened to people who didn't deserve it. Didn't she and her adopted siblings provide enough evidence for that? Granted, the tough times they'd been through had been weathered and her sister and three brothers had all found love with some truly wonderful people. But there was no chance for a happy ending with Alzheimer's disease, and she found herself wishing she could do something for Hunter to ease that pain in his life despite the fact she didn't really know him that well. But she didn't have to be best friends with someone to empathize with him, to wish he had an easier path to travel.

"He seemed to like your photo there." Merline pointed toward the piece that caught the eye as soon as you stepped into the gallery. "I told him he should bring Evelyn to the opening."

"That's a good idea." And it was, but it also made Angel unaccountably nervous. Merline had said he liked the photo of her brother-in-law, Jason, wrestling a steer, but what would he think of the rest of the collection? And why did it seem to matter so much? What was important was that it could provide an enjoyable evening for his mom.

"Maybe you could convince him," Merline said. "I'm not sure I did a very good job."

"I doubt I'd have any more luck than you."

Merline smiled and nodded toward the brownie in Angel's hand. "I'm not so sure about that."

Before Angel could cobble together a response, Merline took her mischievous smile and headed back to her office. Angel looked at the brownie, wondering if Hunter left it for any other reason than the apology he'd attached to it. And wondering why she hoped he had.

By the time Hunter got home, he felt as if he'd sweated off ten pounds up on the gallery roof. He was glad to see Mildred was still visiting with his mom. In fact, when he stepped inside and heard them laughing, he could almost believe everything was as it should be. Especially since he noticed that not only had his mom remembered to dry the clothes but had also folded them. Or had that been Mildred's doing?

He took a moment to listen to the two women sounding like teenagers. He prayed every day that a cure for Alzheimer's disease would be found before it was too late for his mom.

"Hunter, is that you?" his mom called out from the living room.

"Yep." He smiled as he left the laundry area and entered the living room. "What is so funny in here?"

His mom looked at Mildred, and they started laughing again.

"Girl talk," Mildred managed to say as she held her side.

Hunter honestly didn't care what they were talking about as long as it was bringing his mom so much happiness. Not only was her disease slowly chipping away at her, but the accompanying bouts of sadness made his heart ache for her.

When they finally got their laughter under control, his mom looked up at him. "How was your day, dear?"

"Hot, but I got a good amount of work done." Even despite the fact his thoughts had kept drifting to the woman who'd been working in the building below his feet. Angel had still been inside the gallery when he'd called it a day.

"I haven't been by the gallery since right after it opened," Mildred said. "I need to swing by sometime."

"Angel Hartley is having an exhibit opening soon, not sure when. Merline invited me and Mom."

"Oh, I don't think so," his mom said, her smile fading.

"Of course you're going," Mildred said.

When his mom started to object, Mildred waved off the words before they'd even been spoken.

"Hon, yeah, you've got a lousy disease, but it hasn't gotten the best of you yet. I expect more fight out of you than this."

His mom looked surprised by her friend's words, but then miraculously she seemed to accept them and nodded. "I guess it could be fun. What kind of art is it?"

Still stunned that she'd agreed so easily, it took Hunter a moment to remember to respond. "Photography. I saw one of her pieces today. She's really talented."

Not to mention beautiful, but he wasn't going to voice that little fact. Heck, it was obvious to anyone who got within view of Angel.

"And I'll bet her sister-in-law will have some delicious snacks on hand that night," Mildred said.

"Who's her sister-in-law?" his mom asked.

"Lauren Shayne, the Brazos Baker."

"Oh, I like her. She was making the most beautiful cinnamon cupcakes on her show today."

Mildred glanced over at Hunter, and he could tell by her expression that his mom had forgotten that Mildred had already been there when the show aired. Perhaps Mildred had even mentioned that Lauren and Adam Hartley were married now and his mom had forgotten that, as well.

"Though I guess she ought to be called the Blue Falls Baker now," his mom said. "We're a long way from the Brazos."

"She's already got a following with her Brazos moniker, though," Mildred said. "Makes sense to keep it."

"Plus you say *baker* and *Blue Falls* and everyone thinks of Keri Teague," he said, referring to the owner of the Mehlerhaus Bakery on Main Street.

"True," his mom said. "Darn it, now I want cupcakes."

He laughed. "Tell you what, Mom. I'll pick some up before I come home tomorrow. What do you say?"

"I say I raised you right."

They all laughed before Mildred stood to leave.

"Well, I better get home before Henry sends out a search party. Hunter, you find out when Angel's opening is, and we'll all make plans to go."

"Will do," he said as he accompanied her to the door. Once there, he leaned down and gave her a kiss on the cheek. "Thank you for convincing her to go. She never would have agreed if it was just me asking."

Mildred patted his cheek as if he were a little boy, probably because she'd known him since he was born. "Because you're too kindhearted and don't give her the tough love she needs sometimes."

Maybe that was true, but it just seemed wrong when she was still coming to grips with her fate. It wasn't the same as when Mildred had given him some of her tough love when he was a twelve-year-old kid feeling sorry for himself because he'd broken his leg during summer vacation. He could hear what she'd said to him now as clearly as if she'd just uttered the words.

You still got two good arms, don't you?

He smiled, thinking about that long-ago moment that had set him on the path to carving little horses out of scrap pieces of wood he found lying around the ranch. He didn't do it much anymore because he didn't have the time. But whenever he couldn't sleep, he sometimes found some peace in the familiar hobby. In the days right after his mom's diagnosis, he'd carved a dozen of them. They were now all living in a wooden crate out in the barn along with many of his earlier efforts.

"What's that smile for?" Mildred asked.

"Just thankful Mom has such a good friend."

"Well, that's not hard. She's a good woman and she's been there for me on more than one occasion." No doubt she was thinking about when his mom was by her side almost constantly when Mildred's son, Shawn, had been in a terrible accident in high school and they didn't know whether he'd live. Thankfully he had and was now married with three kids, and living in Waco.

After Mildred left, Hunter took a shower and changed into clean clothes before joining his mom in the kitchen. She was just finishing putting dinner on the table, and his stomach rumbled in response.

She laughed. "Sounds like someone worked up an appetite today."

"That I did." For more than just food. Oh, good grief,

he needed to stop thinking about things that couldn't be. How many signs did the universe have to send him that he and Angel Hartley weren't written in the stars?

When they sat down, he took a tentative bite despite how good everything smelled. He figured he was safe from harm since he'd moved all the cleaners and non-food items out of the kitchen and put them in the cabinets above the washer and dryer, but sometimes ingredient mistakes happened. He was happy that his first bite of pork roast was every bit as good as the brownies his mom had made.

"So Angel Hartley, she's the pretty one, right?"

The question was odd considering Sloane was beautiful, too. He just happened to be more attracted to her sister. Good thing since Sloane was now a married woman.

"None of the Hartleys are what I'd call ugly, Mom." Yeah, he could even recognize that the three Hartley sons were handsome guys. And obviously their other halves agreed.

"I know, but Angel's the one you always liked."

He choked on the green beans he'd been chewing. When he managed to get his breath again, the look on his mom's face changed from concern to a knowing smile.

"I don't know where you got that idea," he said.

She lifted a brow. "I know I'm forgetting more and more, but there are things I still remember really well. And the way you've always looked at that girl, I don't know why you haven't asked her out already."

"When do I have time to date?"

"Yes, life is busy, but you know what makes those burdens easier? Someone to share them with."

"I've got you, Mom."

"That's not the same thing and you know it."

Hunter was beginning to think that going to Angel's show opening wasn't the best idea. What if his mom decided to share her theory on his attraction to Angel with the woman in question? Then it wouldn't be his mom standing embarrassed in the middle of the gallery. It'd be him.

Angel hauled the large framed print of a cattle roundup out of the truck, nearly dropping it because of its awkward size.

"Here, let me get that for you."

She looked over to see Hunter quickly approach and grasp the end of the frame.

"Thanks." She scanned their surroundings. "Where did you come from?"

He nodded toward a large tree on the far side of the gallery. "My lunch spot." He took the frame away from her, then stepped back. "After you."

Oddly self-conscious, she led the way toward the gallery. Once inside, she pointed to the front counter.

"You can just set it there."

"I doubt that's its final destination. Where's it going?"

Why in the world was one part of her brain screaming at her to get Hunter out of the gallery as fast as she could while another part wanted him to stay?

"Uh, back wall." She pointed as if he couldn't figure out where that might be.

He carried the heavy framed piece as if it weren't any heavier than an eight-by-ten. After a few steps, he stood in front of the only bare display area left. Since the hanging hardware was already in place, he simply lifted the photo and hung it before stepping to the side.

"How's it look?" he asked.

Perfect, actually. "How did you do that?"

His eyebrows bunched slightly. "Hang a photo?"

"No. Well, yes. I mean you got it perfectly straight on the first go." She gestured at the entirety of the gallery's showroom. "I had to make no less than half a dozen attempts on every one of these before they were right."

Hunter glanced at the piece he'd hung. "Beginner's luck, I guess."

"So you're a picture-hanging expert, roofer, rancher and gifter of brownies. Is there a jack-of-all-trades competition going on that I'm not aware of?"

Hunter smiled at that, and Angel mentally added great smiles to his list of attributes. Seriously, had he always possessed that smile? If so, why was there not a pantie shortage in Blue Falls because every woman had tossed hers at Hunter like he was a rock star? She suddenly became very aware of the pair of blue cotton panties she was wearing. Not exactly sexy, but that hadn't been a concern for quite some time. And she wasn't planning on showing them to anyone. Still, Hunter's smile had made her think about them.

"If there is such a competition, Bernie Shumaker would win. I hear his latest venture is selling painted rocks online."

She laughed. "You know, one day he's going to hit on something and strike it rich while the rest of us are still working our tails off."

"You're probably right." He glanced around them. "Though he's probably not the only one on the way to striking it rich."

"That's nice of you to say, but I'll be satisfied with being able to pay the bills." Which wasn't exactly true. She daydreamed of becoming a success, maybe even so noted that her work graced the covers of magazines and earned spots in top-notch Western galleries. But first things first. She wanted this local show to be a success.

He gave her another smile, but this one seemed to say that he suspected she was just being modest. Did he want more from his life than ranching and working on hot roofs? She suddenly wanted to know what those dreams might be.

Hunter walked over to another of her photos, this one of a barrel racer as she rounded a barrel, her face reflecting her drive to post a fast time.

"You're really talented."

"Thank you." People had told her that before, but something about the way he said it, like he was looking at a painting by one of the great masters, caused warmth to fill her chest.

"How did you get started?"

She took a few steps until she was standing beside him, gazing at her work. "I've liked taking photos for as long as I can remember. With the ranch right out the front door, I guess I just gravitated naturally toward the subject."

He pointed at the photo in front of them. "What about the rodeo shots?"

"I started taking a few at the local rodeos and became determined to get the best shots possible. It's not easy considering how fast the action is. I have to weed through hundreds of unusable photos to find a single one that I'd be willing to put my name on."

"I guess this exhibit is the result of lots of hours of work, then."

"You have no idea. It's like I'm never truly done, not like hauling a load of cattle to market. There is no finish, not when there is more to photograph, ways to continually improve, brainstorming about new directions to try. Arden, Neil's wife, says it's the same with writing. You're always *on*."

"You could say the same about ranching. One task or season always flows into the next."

"That's true. Still, it's different."

"I'll take your word for it."

The sound of the front door opening drew their attention. In came Merline, making Angel aware that she hadn't even thought about whether the other woman had been in the building.

"Hey, you two," Merline said as she approached. "Oh, that last piece looks wonderful."

"Thanks. I sure hope someone buys it because I don't want to lug it back home. I got lucky that your roofer was here to lend a hand." Angel gave Hunter a smile she hoped conveyed her gratitude.

He gave her a slight nod.

"So, will we see you and your mom at the opening?" Merline asked Hunter.

He glanced at Angel with an expression she couldn't pinpoint before answering. "Yeah, if she's feeling up to it."

"Great. It'll be nice to see Evelyn."

After Merline headed for her office, Hunter said, "I better get back to work."

"Hunter, I wanted to thank you for the brownie yesterday. It really hit the spot."

"Good. Mom made them."

"I'm glad you're bringing her to the opening." She tried not to believe she felt that way for selfish reasons.

Hunter looked surprised by her words but then shifted

his gaze toward one of her photos. "I hope it's the right thing to do."

Before she could figure what to say in response, he headed toward the exit. As he opened the door, he stepped to the side to let someone else in. Angel jerked her gaze away from Hunter when she realized the person stepping inside was Lauren, her newest sister-in-law.

"Who was that?" Lauren asked as she came near and gestured over her shoulder.

"Hunter Millbrook. He's working on the roof." As if to provide evidence she was telling the truth, she heard the thump of his footsteps above their heads.

"Huh. I had an entire restaurant reroofed and I have to say none of the roofers looked that fine."

"And here I thought you only had eyes for my brother."

"I wasn't noting the man's hotness for my own benefit. Seems like the last unattached Hartley might be smitten."

Angel waved away Lauren's too-close-to-the-truth observation. "You're not a credible judge. You're still floating around in the newlywed fog."

"Be that as it may, I still trust my eyes. And they saw you checking out the roofer's rear view."

Angel rolled her eyes. "I suppose I should have expected this. With the rest of my siblings married off now, Mom has set her sights on me and recruited you to her cause."

"Actually, no. She hasn't said a word to me or Adam."

That surprised Angel, but maybe it shouldn't. While Neil, Ben, Sloane and Adam had all been the target of teasing about pairing up, it was as if the family had a moratorium on doing the same to her. In an odd way, it was nice that Lauren hadn't gotten the memo and treated her like a normal person, one who didn't have a history of being abandoned by the people who were supposed to love her.

"Listen," Lauren said. "I'm the expert on not wanting to get involved with anyone after being done wrong, so hopefully you'll trust me when I say the asses in our pasts aren't worth forfeiting our opportunities for happiness."

"Do I seem unhappy?"

"No, not really. But I also know what it's like to hide what I'm really feeling from the people around me. And having the support and love of family is great, but it's not the same as being in love."

"Well, I wouldn't say a bit of innocent ogling is being in love."

Lauren smiled. "But sometimes it leads to it."

Angel held up her hand. "Please don't go into detail about you ogling Adam's butt or something."

Lauren laughed. "Well, actually—"

Angel put her hands over her ears. "I'm not listening."

Lauren shook her head and pulled a piece of paper out of her purse. "Fine, be a spoilsport. I came by to see what you think about these for your opening."

Angel accepted the list of food items. "I told you I trusted you, cooking being your area of expertise and all."

"Yes, but it's still your big night. I'd hate to have something out that makes you want to gag."

"As long as there isn't any peanut butter, you're golden."

"That's still weird, not liking peanut butter without being allergic to it."

"It's nasty, end of story."

After they settled on the refreshment menu and Lauren left, Angel sank onto a bench facing the large roundup photo. Setting aside the teasing, she considered Lauren's words. If Lauren could get past what her ex-fiancé had done to her—trying to cheat her out of her business and denying his twin daughters were even his—maybe there was hope for Angel to find love again.

She ran her hand over her face. Why was she even thinking about love a mere day after she realized she was attracted to Hunter? Shouldn't she perhaps think about casual dating first? Had she not learned her lesson about falling head over heels too quickly? That hadn't turned out so well last time. Were it not for Julia, it would have been a total disaster.

Julia. The thought of her daughter caused her to take a mental step back. Angel had deliberately not gotten too involved with anyone since the birth of her daughter to protect Julia in every way a mother could protect her child.

Maybe she was just feeling lonely and left out now that all her brothers and sister were happily married. They had someone to wake up next to each morning, someone with whom to share intimacy. Loneliness had made its presence known now and then since the day she'd told Dave she was pregnant and he'd responded by saying he didn't want to be a father and promptly leaving town. It had been as if she'd been kicked in the heart. Again, someone who'd claimed to love her had chosen abandoning her instead of sticking around. When you started out life being left at a hospital by your birth mother with only a blanket and a short note, trust wasn't automatically given. To have the man who'd claimed to love her take off for parts unknown... Well, that didn't help.

She snorted lightly. Dave hadn't been a man. He'd been an immature boy who wanted the fun of sex without the responsibility of the baby that resulted. She'd wager money she couldn't afford that he was still that immature ass.

Even knowing all that, something about Lauren and Adam's wedding the month before, coinciding with the big grand opening of her Brazos Baker Barbecue restaurant, had caused the loneliness that made only periodic appearances to take up seemingly permanent residence within Angel.

Not wanting to think about Dave or her unattached status anymore, she headed to Merline's office.

"You finished, hon?" Merline asked when she looked up from her desk.

"For today. All that's left to do is get some small matted prints of the bigger pieces ready. I'll bring those by tomorrow."

Angel thought about walking straight to the truck without acknowledging Hunter, but that felt rude somehow. So she shaded her eyes as she looked up to where he stood on the roof.

"Don't melt up there."

He smiled, making it more likely she was the one who might melt.

"No promises."

All the way back to the Rocking Horse Ranch, that smile and her zingy reaction to it kept replaying in her mind—along with the thought that it was odd how you could know someone for years and then one day suddenly see them in an entirely different light.

And how that realization left you at a complete loss for what you were going to do about it. Or if you should do nothing at all.

Chapter 3

Hunter finished putting his tools in his truck before giving the roof a final once-over. Not bad if he did say so himself. Those summers of working on a roofing crew when he was in high school came in handy when he needed to make extra money, which seemed to be all the time.

Though he needed to be back at the ranch to catch up on work there, he'd miss seeing Angel. Even if it was just in passing. It was likely for the best, however, that he be removed from seeing her too often. Even if she could be interested in him as a man, he wouldn't blame her for not wanting to get involved when all he could offer was a hardscrabble ranch and years of his mom's declining health. Angel seemed to be on the cusp of big things in her career, and who knew where that might take her. He wasn't about to even consider standing in the way of that journey.

Refocusing his attention on what really mattered, he headed toward the gallery to get paid for his work.

"All done?" Merline asked as he stepped into the cooler interior.

"Yes, ma'am. Your roof shouldn't cause you any more problems."

"How are you at painting?"

Her question surprised him, but the prospect of more income was welcome. "I've done my share."

"Do you have time to repaint the gazebo, the benches in the garden and the fence around the edge of the lot?"

He weighed the hours needed to complete those tasks, hours he'd have to be away from his mom, against how much he'd make. "I do."

"Great. How quickly can you get it done? I was hoping to have the place looking all freshened up by Angel's opening."

He realized the painting might have the additional benefit of more opportunities to be around Angel. And despite the knowledge that not seeing her was probably the wiser course, he couldn't deny that he really liked the idea of more opportunities to talk to her. "I can make that happen."

She patted him on the arm, how he imagined she might with her own sons. Which made him wonder...

"If you don't mind me asking, why aren't you having Nathan or Ryan do it?" Heck, even Simon wasn't busy with his sheriff's duties all the time.

"Those boys are going ten different directions if they're going one. No telling when they'd get around to it."

Hunter knew that feeling, but he was thankful it applied to the Teague men, as well. That meant the painting job would fall to him and help fill the Millbrook coffers. And even though nothing would likely come of it, he'd accept the opportunity to spend more time around Angel. He'd deal with the inevitable withdrawal symptoms when they were both back to their normal lives on opposite sides of the county.

"You'll never guess who I ran into in town today," Diane Hartley said as she turned away from the refrigerator where she'd been stowing leftovers following dinner.

Angel glanced at her mom before loading more dishes into the dishwasher. "No idea."

For a tense moment, Angel wondered if her mom was going to say Hunter's name. Angel had been trying to stop thinking about him since she left the gallery—with zero success.

"Chris Ross. I always liked him. Made me sad when you two broke up."

"Are you kidding?" Sloane said as she deposited the last of the dirty dishes in front of Angel. "He was such a little—"

Angel met her sister's eyes and mentally filled in what Sloane had been about to say but had stopped for their mom's benefit.

"Why would you say that?" Diane asked.

"Because he went out with someone else while we were dating." Angel didn't reveal the whole truth—that by "went out with someone else" she meant "slept with someone else."

"Oh, I'm so sorry, honey," her mom said as she placed a comforting hand on Angel's arm. "I had no idea."

"No need to apologize. It was forever ago, and it wasn't as if we'd been going out for ages."

Sure, five months, but still, when you compared it with something like Lauren had been through—or even what Angel later experienced with Dave—it didn't matter that much. But it had hurt at the time and was yet another failure in Angel's relationship history. If she had any sense, she'd give up on men forever. But it was so hard not to want the kind of happiness and connection she saw her siblings enjoying with their spouses, the same type of deep devotion that her parents had to one another.

If only she could be sure everything would work out—for her sake and her daughter's.

Her mom looked as if she might be about to say something else before she clamped down on whatever it was and instead escorted her grandchildren out to the backyard to play with Maggie, the family's Australian shepherd.

"You know she's dying to find someone for you," Sloane said as she leaned back against the sink.

"I know. I'm honestly surprised she's holding herself in check. If she married me off, she'd have a complete set."

"I think she blames herself for what happened with Dave."

Angel stopped halfway to loading a dirty plate into the dishwasher. "What? That makes no sense."

"In her mind it does. She feels she should have seen the signs, should have warned you, protected you."

"It was my fault for trusting the wrong guy. I seem to be good at that."

"Don't."

"What? Tell the truth? You can't deny my dating history is full of epic failures."

"You're not alone in that."

Angel winced. Of course, she wasn't. Sloane and Lauren were proof enough of that fact. "Sorry."

"I wasn't fishing for sympathy or an apology. Just pointing out that no matter what happened in the past, the future isn't written yet. You can make it whatever you want—with whomever you want."

Angel's thoughts went right to Hunter, which made about as much sense as her mom blaming herself for Angel's failed romances.

"Um, what is that look?" Sloane pointed toward Angel's face, apparently seeing more than Angel had intended.

She pretended she didn't notice and wiped at her cheek. "Do I have food on my face?"

"No, you have 'I have a guy in mind' on your face."

"I do not." Angel made a dismissive sound and went back to loading the dishwasher.

"Who is he?"

"There is no *he*. You're imagining things."

"No, pretty sure I'm not, and rest assured, I'll get the information out of you eventually."

Angel's thoughts shifted to how Lauren had teased her about Hunter at the gallery. But based on Sloane's questions, Lauren hadn't said anything. At least nothing specific.

"Can't get what's not there."

"Deny it all you want, but I know what I saw."

"Believe whatever you want. I can't stop you."

"It's okay to just have a little fun, you know. If you're not ready for a relationship, you can just, shall we say, scratch an itch."

Angel's mouth dropped open as she stared at her sister. "Did you seriously just encourage me to go out and get laid by the first guy I come across?"

"Maybe not the *first* guy, especially if he's really unappealing. Or married."

Angel rolled her eyes, closed the dishwasher and started the cycle.

"All I'm saying is that you've spent the entirety of Julia's life alone. She's in school now, and you deserve something for yourself. Someone to get the blood pumping."

Well, the sight of Hunter Millbrook's ass encased in those worn jeans had accomplished that already, but she wasn't about to tell Sloane that piece of information. If she gave any sort of signal that she was ready to enter the dating world again, Angel knew she would be opening the floodgates of matchmaking. When she did take that step, she'd like to navigate her own path. No suggestions from her well-meaning mother. No endless teasing from her siblings. No getting on the radar of Blue Falls matchmaker Verona Charles, who, despite finally finding a love of her own in Lauren's grandfather, still persisted in doing her best to play Cupid.

At the sound of Sloane's laughter, Angel looked over at her sister.

"I don't know how you ever kept anything away from Mom and Dad," Sloane said. "I can see right through you."

"Don't you have a husband you can go home to and bother instead?"

"If my little sister is up to babysitting her nephew, maybe I'll go scratch an itch of my own."

"There are just some things I don't need to know."

Sloane laughed again as she backed toward the door. "But you'll keep Brent tonight?"

"You know I will, despite you being highly annoying."

"Thanks, sis. And when you're ready, I'll watch Julia."

In the quiet that descended on the kitchen after Sloane's departure, Angel dared let herself fantasize just a little bit about what it might be like to spend some *adult* time with Hunter. Some itch-scratching hours free of responsibility. The mere thought made her squirm, so she headed for the back door and three things sure to push lustful thoughts out of her head—a hyper dog playing catch, two energetic children and her mother.

But as she sank onto the bench of one of the picnic tables and watched the kids playing, damned if images of Hunter Millbrook smiling down at her from that hot roof didn't plague her as if she were alone and allowing her fantasies free rein.

Hunter placed the cans of paint and assorted supplies on the counter at the hardware store.

"That be all for ya?" Daria Winton asked from behind the cash register.

"Yes, ma'am."

She chuckled. "Save the *ma'am* stuff for someone older than you."

He smiled, remembering that Daria had been a year behind him in school.

Her gaze darted to his left, and her eyes lit up. "Hey, Chris. I heard you were back in town."

Hunter glanced over to find a full-grown version of Chris Ross standing next to him, a basket full of assorted items in hand. He hadn't seen Chris in years; he had heard he'd gone to college in Oregon and hadn't come back. But now here he stood, a younger version of his father. That he'd bump into Chris now, right when all the roads his thoughts were taking led back to Angel, seemed like a giant flashing sign from the universe. What it was saying, he had no idea. Probably that he needed to stop thinking about Angel so much.

"Yeah."

Odd, he remembered Chris being a lot more talkative, not that he wanted to strike up a conversation or anything. Maybe Chris just wasn't a morning person.

"Hunter, right?" Chris said when he made eye contact.

Hunter nodded.

"Looks like you're going to be doing some painting, too."

Hunter noticed that in addition to the basket Chris held, he also had a can of paint in the other hand. "Helping out your parents?"

Chris shook his head. "Rented a place out toward Poppy. Needs some fixing up."

"You're moving back to Blue Falls?" Even though he knew Chris and Angel had broken up years ago, it still felt like odd timing for Hunter to run into one of Angel's exes right after his attraction to her had received a boost.

Some hint of emotion passed over Chris's face, and Hunter had the impression it was sorrow. He hadn't heard of anything being wrong with Chris's parents or his younger sister, but he wasn't exactly one to keep tabs on everyone else's lives, either. He had plenty to manage in his own.

"For now, at least."

Hunter experienced the strangest urge to ask if Chris was okay, but he refrained. They'd never been friends. He would barely call them acquaintances.

Daria's voice telling Hunter his total broke the awkward moment, and he handed over the money. When she returned his change, Hunter glanced at Chris and nodded.

"See ya."

"Yeah."

See ya? He didn't really want to see Chris again, but it was something you said when it was too rude to simply walk away without a word. Even so, he couldn't get the fleeting expression he'd seen on Chris's face out of his mind for some reason. By the time he pulled into the parking lot for the gallery, he realized how Chris had really looked—haunted.

That didn't fit at all with what he remembered about Chris, but then people changed. Life changed them. It still didn't mean he hoped the guy crossed paths with Angel, but he could at least accept that maybe Chris— like everyone else in the world—had things to deal with that no one else knew about.

But that wasn't Hunter's concern. The job that lay before him was.

A couple of vehicles sat in the lot, but neither belonged to Angel. Maybe she was done with preparing her exhibit and this extra work he'd agreed to do wouldn't provide him with any further opportunities to see or talk with her after all. His mood dampened when he considered that he might have to wait until the exhibit opening, and no doubt she'd be so busy she wouldn't be able to spare him more than a passing "Hello, thanks for coming."

He grabbed his supplies and headed toward the garden area at the corner of the property. Frustration gnawed at him as he stared at the chipped paint on the top of the wooden fence. He needed to stop thinking about Angel and focus on his work. And that was what he managed to do for the next couple of hours, working up a sweat as the heat of the day built. It wasn't as hot as it had been up on the roof, but he would still appreciate a shower at the end of the day.

"It's looking good."

All it took was a single three-word sentence in that familiar voice to shove everything else right out of his brain. Doing his best not to grin like a fool, he turned to see Angel standing there in a tank top and shorts that revealed so much of her smooth skin that for a moment he felt light-headed. And here he stood sweaty and dirty. Yeah, a real catch.

She laughed, pulling him firmly back to earth.

"What?"

Angel motioned toward her upper lip. "You appear to have given yourself half a white mustache."

He wiped at his lip.

"No, the other side."

He switched the wet paintbrush to his opposite hand and reached up to the area she indicated. A few specks of gooey paint peeled away, but he could tell most of it had dried already.

"Dang it," he said under his breath, hating that he probably looked like an idiot. "I was swatting at a bee earlier. Guess I painted myself in the process."

"It gives you a bit of the absentminded artist look."

"Oh, great. Just what I wanted." Having Angel Hartley laugh at him wasn't exactly the reaction he'd dreamed about.

"Hey, there's nothing wrong with looking like an artist," she said.

"No, I didn't mean that," he said, worried that he'd offended her. "It's the absentminded part that I'd like to avoid."

She appeared suddenly horrified, and he wondered why until he realized she must know about his mom's illness and thought he was making some sort of connection to it. A wave of guilt hit him that his mother had been the furthest thing from his mind as he considered how he looked in Angel's eyes.

"Don't look so worried."

"I didn't think," she said.

"Neither did I."

Angel seemed like she didn't quite believe him.

"Honestly." To move them away from the topic, he motioned toward the gallery. "Almost ready for your opening?"

Her expression changed, this time to reflect a hint of anxiety. "As ready as I'm going to be, I guess. I'm setting up the matted prints, a cheaper option for people if they're interested but can't afford an original."

"Sounds like a good idea."

"You're still attending, right?"

He tried not to read too much into her question. Likely she was just anxious about people showing up, and he and his mom would be at least two warm bodies.

"That's the plan. Guess I'll have to try on my suit and see if it still fits." He tried not to think about how the last time he'd worn it had been at his father's funeral. It was probably out of style now, and his body had changed from his more awkward late-teens frame.

"No need to wear a suit," she said. "We're still in Blue Falls after all."

"Oh. I've never been to an art opening before." He'd assumed they were fancy shindigs, and he felt the opposite of fancy.

"Well, you certainly don't need to stress out about it. That's my job."

"Why are you stressed out?"

She shrugged. "I guess I've just put so much into this that I want it to be a success."

"And you don't think it will be?"

"No idea. Art is subjective. What one person likes, another might think is total garbage."

"I might not be an art expert, but your photos are far from garbage. They're fantastic."

Fantastic? When had he ever used that word to describe anything? It actually felt weird coming out of his mouth. But the wide-eyed look of appreciation gracing Angel's face made it his new favorite word.

"You really think so?"

He hated hearing her sound so uncertain.

"Positive. I guess we're all our own worst critics."

She nodded. "That's what Lauren says."

"So is she providing refreshments for your opening? My mom and Mildred Hopkins were nearly bouncing at the idea."

Angel smiled, causing an extra beat of his heart. "She is. What does your mom like?"

"I'm sure anything will be great."

"You're right, but does your mom have any favorites?"

Something expanded within him at the idea that she'd

even think to have something special on hand for his mom. "Orange is her favorite flavor."

Angel nodded. "I'll see what Lauren can come up with."

"This is your night. You should have what you want."

"I'm one hundred percent positive that I'll be too nervous to eat anything. Plus, it's a special night out for your mom. And I'm sure everyone else will like whatever Lauren makes."

"Thank you." His throat felt thick with emotion.

"What about you? Any favorites?"

"I'm not picky."

"Neither are my brothers, for the most part, but they still have favorites."

"Chocolate, I guess."

She lifted an eyebrow. "You guess?"

"Okay, definitely chocolate. I wouldn't throw caramel out the front door, either."

"Duly noted," she said. "Well, I guess I better let you get back to work and do my own."

The last thing he wanted was for her to leave, but he didn't know how to convey that without looking embarrassingly desperate.

He forced himself to turn back toward the fence as she headed for the gallery.

"Oh, and, Hunter?"

He looked back to where she was facing him again, a grin tugging at her mouth that was full of unexpected mischief.

"No suit for the opening, but you might want to make sure you don't have half a paint mustache." She grinned. "Or at least paint the other side to match."

He laughed—a laugh so real that he realized he couldn't remember the last time it had happened. As he watched Angel turn and head inside, he knew what he had to do. No matter what else was going on in his life, he had to at least try to find a way to make Angel Hartley a part of it.

Chapter 4

Angel looked at herself in the mirror for what had to be the hundredth time in the past hour and decided the black dress wasn't right, either. It was as if she was experiencing her day in the gallery when everything looked crooked all over again, only with her wardrobe.

Why was she stressing so much about what to wear to her exhibit opening anyway? After all, there was no guarantee anyone would even show up. Although with Lauren providing the refreshments, perhaps at least she'd draw a few of her sister-in-law's fans.

She sank onto the edge of her bed, which was piled with darn near every piece of clothing from her closet. What she'd told Hunter—that a suit wasn't necessary, this being Blue Falls—replayed in her head, and yet here she sat completely twisted up in knots about her own outfit. Granted, it was her exhibit, but still.

A knock at the door drew her attention away from the full-length mirror.

"Yeah?"

Her mom poked her head in. "Okay in here?"

Angel sighed. "Sure, if by 'okay' you mean I'm at the stage where I'm considering wearing my oldest jeans and rattiest T-shirt. Really go for the just-came-from-mucking-out-the-stalls look."

No one was going to buy a photo based on how well she was dressed anyway, right?

Her mom opened the door farther and stepped inside. "You're putting too much pressure on yourself, sweetie. You know people love your photos."

Sure, she'd made some positive steps in her career, but it didn't keep her from expecting it to all just disappear if she made one wrong move.

"I really don't know why I'm so nervous."

"It's because you feel as if you'll be on display, that you as a person are being judged instead of your work."

Angel started to argue but stopped herself when she realized her mom might be onto something. Was that why she'd gravitated toward photography—because it pointed people's attention away from her? By having an exhibit opening, she was inviting their attention back toward her.

"I think you really missed your calling, Mom. You could have been one heck of a therapist."

Her mom laughed. "Honey, all moms are therapists."

Angel considered the times she'd listened when Julia had been upset about something, how she'd done her best to help her daughter learn how to deal with her emotions.

"I don't know how you did it five times over."

"I like a challenge." Her mom motioned for Angel to

stand. "That dress is perfect. All it needs is a little accessorizing."

Angel watched as her mom walked over to the dresser and opened the wooden jewelry box Ben had made for Angel last Christmas. When she turned back toward Angel, she was holding a turquoise necklace and earring set Angel had bought herself the first time she'd sold a photo to a national magazine. Even though she had no idea what tribe she'd been born a part of, she'd nevertheless always been attracted to Native American jewelry. She had managed to amass a collection of everything from Navajo turquoise and silver to Cherokee carved-bone pieces to a pewter raven necklace made by a Tlingit artist. She wasn't sure if it was some sort of search for her heritage or she just liked the designs. Maybe both.

She accepted the jewelry from her mom and quickly put it on. When she looked in the mirror again, she was happier with what she saw than at any point during her entire crazed afternoon. She made eye contact with her mom's reflection.

"Do you ever get tired of being right?"

Her mom chuckled. "Nope. And don't be surprised if I remind you that you said that somewhere down the line."

Angel wondered if her mom was talking about matchmaking, but then she remembered what Sloane had said about her mom feeling guilty about what had happened with Dave. She opened her mouth to tell her mom there was no need for her to feel that way, but the words wouldn't come. As if to save her from standing there with her mouth wide-open, Julia appeared in the open doorway.

"Well, don't you look beautiful," Diane said.

Angel agreed and it hit her how much older her daughter looked than she had, seemingly, only the day before. She'd even insisted on dressing herself in the room that had once been Sloane's and had recently become Julia's very own space. No more sharing with Angel. Though part of Angel liked having more privacy, she couldn't deny she missed having Julia so close at the same time. After all, they'd shared a room from the moment Julia had been born. But she understood how exciting it was for Julia to have a room that was hers and hers alone.

"My little girl is growing up."

Julia giggled. "I'm only in first grade, Mom."

Even that fact highlighted how fast the past six years had flown by. If she wasn't careful, Angel was going to blink and Julia would be driving and asking permission to go out on a date. She almost snorted thinking about how many layers of Hartleys a boy was going to have to get through before he was given permission to even meet Julia at a school dance, let alone go on an actual date where they'd be alone together. *Gauntlet* was probably the right word for it. Julia loved being surrounded by loads of family now, but Angel wondered if that attitude might change with the passage of years.

"Well, we all better get going or we're going to be late," Angel's mom said as she ushered Julia out the doorway.

Angel's nerves came back full force, so she inhaled a deep breath while taking one final look in the mirror. Amid all the worry that the opening would be a stunning failure, an entirely different concern bubbled up. Would Hunter think she looked nice?

"Oh, good grief," she whispered to her reflection and shook her head.

"What, honey?" her mom asked.

"Nothing."

Nothing but crazy thoughts coming from my crazy brain.

When they arrived at the gallery, there were only a couple of cars in the lot and Angel's stomach sank until she reminded herself that it was still early. The start time wasn't for a half hour yet, so it made sense that only Merline's and Lauren's cars were there already. She wished she could see into the future, to how things would go tonight. If she was worrying for no reason, she'd like to know so she could calm the heck down.

She held Julia's hand as they walked into the gallery. Angel's gaze went directly to the table filled with delectable treats provided by Lauren and her sister, Violet.

"Are you trying to outshine me? Because that looks like an art display all on its own," she said as she pointed at the array of bite-size appetizers, cakes and tarts.

"If attendees like the treats, they stay longer and are in a better mood. A better mood may loosen their purse strings and wallets."

"I like how you think."

Lauren smiled. "Hon, even if I'd brought prepackaged snacks, it wouldn't have mattered. Your work is great. Your show is going to be a big success."

"From your lips to God's ears."

Gradually, people began to trickle in, and chatting with each one helped Angel to breathe a little easier. It didn't mean she'd sell anything, but at least she wouldn't be standing around in an empty gallery stuffing her face with all of Lauren's tasty treats.

Julia tugged on her hand, drawing Angel's attention

away from greeting Nathan and Grace Teague, Merline's oldest son and his wife.

"Mom, can I have some cake? Aunt Lauren said I had to ask you." The pleading in her daughter's eyes almost made Angel laugh.

"Sure, sweetie, but no more than a couple." Angel caught Lauren's attention and held up two fingers to indicate Julia could have only two of the bite-size treats. Any more than that and she'd be bouncing off the walls until way past her bedtime.

When Julia headed back toward her aunt, Angel called out, "And don't get anywhere near the photographs."

Violet smiled from behind the refreshment table and indicated they'd keep an eye on Julia.

Over the next several minutes, Angel put on her best cool and collected face as she chatted with friends and strangers alike. She was discussing her views on various cameras with a couple from Austin when she caught sight of Hunter entering the gallery with his mother and completely forgot what she was saying.

He'd followed her advice and left the suit at home, but the blue shirt he wore sent sparks of attraction racing along her skin. She couldn't even really say why. It was the type of nice button-down that any number of men owned, but for some reason on Hunter it looked like the sexiest piece of clothing she'd ever seen. The only thing that would make it sexier would be if he unbuttoned the cuffs and rolled up the sleeves to expose his lower arms. She might have a thing for arms.

"Is everything all right?"

She visibly startled at the question that came from the man in front of her.

"I'm terribly sorry. I saw someone I know come in. You were saying?"

As the man resumed the conversation, Angel had a difficult time not letting her gaze wander, especially when the man's wife looked toward Hunter and gave Angel a knowing grin.

When the conversation came to a natural conclusion, Angel searched the crowd for Hunter and his mom. When she spotted them talking to Sloane, she nearly sprinted across the gallery as alarm bells clanged so loudly in her head she was surprised they weren't audible to anyone else. But before she could take the first step toward making sure her sister wasn't in the midst of mortifying her, Merline was at her side, steering her in the opposite direction.

"You need to meet someone," Merline said as they approached a middle-aged man wearing a dark suit and a bolo tie with a silver longhorn. "Angel Hartley, this is Steven Hill. He works for *West* magazine."

As she shook Steven's hand, Angel hoped he couldn't sense her nervousness. Was she actually shaking? She couldn't tell. How many times had she imagined her work gracing the glossy pages of his magazine? But the competition was stiff, not unlike a *National Geographic* for Western landscapes and people.

"It's very nice to meet you," she said, wondering how he'd come to be in a small Hill Country town.

As they talked, she learned the answer was he liked to check out local galleries whenever his family vacationed and they were enjoying some river recreation on the Frio River over in Poppy. Angel couldn't believe her luck.

Of course, there was no guarantee, but at least he took one of her business cards and seemed interested as he listened to her answer his questions about how she got her start, her inspiration and vision for her career.

After he left, she desperately wanted to sit down. But the gallery's two benches were already full.

"Please tell me I didn't stammer through that like a complete idiot."

Merline squeezed her hand. "Far from it."

Angel hoped Merline was right because entry into *West* magazine would make this night a huge success even if she didn't sell any photographs at all.

As Merline turned to talk to other patrons, Angel walked toward the refreshment table, needing an infusion of sugar. She'd just popped a mini lemon concoction that tasted like heaven in her mouth when she turned to find Hunter only an arm's length away.

"Good turnout tonight," he said.

She tried to smile and acknowledge his statement without opening her full mouth.

"Sorry," he said with a smile before moving to the table and snagging one of the chocolate squares Lauren had flavored with orange, a mixture that combined the flavors Hunter had claimed were his and his mother's favorites. "These are delicious," he said to Lauren. "Everything is."

"Thank you," Lauren replied. "Nothing but the best for our talented photographer."

Angel managed to swallow her dessert before Hunter turned back to her. "Is your mom having a nice time?"

Just looking at Evelyn Millbrook, you'd never know she had such a devastating disease.

"She was nervous about coming, but she seems to have calmed down since we got here. She likes your work."

"I'm glad she came."

"Me, too."

Angel scrambled for some way to keep their conversation going, thinking back over their previous ones. "So, uh, what do you think of your first art exhibit opening?"

"It's more socializing than I'm used to, but it has some perks." He held up his dessert.

She scanned the room, wondering how many of the people filling it would be there if Lauren wasn't providing the refreshments.

Hunter leaned into her field of view. "I'm kidding. It's actually nice to get out, and I'm glad so many people showed up for your big night."

"Yeah, it would have been a tragedy if we had to eat all of Lauren's food by ourselves."

Hunter laughed a little. "Yeah, a real tragedy."

The front door opened to admit someone else. It took Angel a moment to recognize Chris Ross. What the devil was he doing at her opening?

Hunter shifted beside her. "I better go check on Mom."

She reached out as if to stop him, but he was already out of reach. Could he possibly think she'd rather talk to Chris than him? But really, why did he have any reason to think otherwise? He had no clue she'd developed a sudden attraction to him, and she doubted he had any in-depth knowledge of her past relationship with Chris beyond perhaps knowing they dated. She wanted to grab Hunter and disavow him of any potential notions that she wanted to get back with Chris.

She pressed her palm against her forehead. *Come on.* Chances were he wasn't thinking about her and Chris at all. Maybe his departure from her side was as simple as his wanting to check on his mom. After all, he'd said she'd been nervous about attending.

And the truth was that she probably shouldn't be feeling any more yearning for Hunter than she was for Chris. As she'd told Sloane, her experience with men didn't leave her with much confidence that getting involved with them was worth the potential heartache.

Before she could make her way to talk to someone else in the room—anyone—Chris made eye contact, smiled and headed toward her. Great, just what she needed to kill the delightful—if potentially unwise—buzz spending time with Hunter had given her.

"Hey, Angel," Chris said as he drew near, sounding tentative in a way she'd never heard from him before. Maybe the grown-up version of Chris realized just how crappy his teenage self had been to her.

Angel wasn't really interested in being a part of some apology tour, but she couldn't exactly be rude to him in the current circumstances. Plus, it wasn't as if she was upset with him anymore. He hadn't destroyed some great love affair after proclaiming his undying affection.

"Hi, Chris. Been a long time."

He nodded. "I just recently moved back."

And if she wasn't mistaken, he didn't seem overly excited by that fact.

He gestured toward the rest of the room. "Pretty awesome you have your own exhibit. I remember how much you used to like taking pictures."

She was honestly surprised he remembered anything about her.

"If you'll excuse me, I need to play hostess." Maybe she sounded rude, but she felt weird engaging in small talk with an old boyfriend with Hunter in the vicinity. And yes, that was probably all kinds of nutty, because there was nothing between her and Hunter beyond casual conversations.

"Wait." Chris suddenly looked exponentially more uncomfortable than he had moments before. "I'd like to take you to lunch sometime."

"I don't think that's a good idea, do you?"

"Just as friends." She must have given him an incredulous look because he quickly corrected himself. "Okay, former classmates? I just want to talk, onetime deal and I promise not to keep you long."

She wanted to decline yet again, but there was something profoundly honest in the way he asked. An honesty she would have never ascribed to him. Curiosity about this seemingly new version of Chris had her going against her initial response and agreeing to meet for lunch at some future date.

"Thanks." He sounded so sincere, like he'd fully expected her to tell him no but was grateful she hadn't.

Seriously, what was going on? Why all of a sudden was she seeing former high school classmates in a different light?

Sloane appeared at her side, and Angel could feel the throttle-the-guy vibes coming off her sister like waves of sound from the bass speakers at a rock concert. Before Sloane could say anything, Chris was pulled into conversation with Jake Monroe.

"What did he want?"

"I'm not actually sure, other than to meet for lunch and talk."

"You told him no, of course."

"I was going to, but I changed my mind."

"That or you've lost it."

"It's no big deal. I'm not going to date him again after

all, but there was just something... I don't know, something different and kind of sad maybe." Sloane pulled a look of disbelief. "I know, I know. But what happened between us was ages ago. I'm not the same person I was then. Maybe he isn't, either."

"But what about Hunter?"

Angel winced and looked around, fearing Hunter might be right behind her again. "Could you please keep your voice down?"

"I knew it! You've got the hots for him."

"Do you honestly think I'd tell you if I did?"

"Yes, eventually, because I'd become such a pest you'd tell me just to shut me up."

Angel stared at her older sister for a moment before sighing. "That's unfortunately true."

"Did you just admit I'm right?"

"Will it indeed shut up you?"

"I'd say yes, but then I'd be lying."

Angel exhaled in frustration.

"Oh, come on, don't be like that." Sloane started to turn in Hunter's direction, but Angel grabbed her arm to stay her.

"Don't make a big deal out of nothing. I happened to notice he's not exactly bad-looking, that's all."

"Not exactly bad-looking? I think the word you're searching for is *hot*."

He was that, but she wasn't going to give Sloane the satisfaction of hearing her admit it.

"I need to go talk to people, try to drum up some sales."

"Avoid me all you want. I know where you live."

Angel rolled her eyes as she deliberately moved to a section of the gallery that put several layers of people between her and Hunter. Because her sister was likely watching her every move.

Though she wasn't sure if any of the framed pieces had sold yet, she was happy to see several of the matted prints had. Despite suspecting that Sloane was watching her, Angel couldn't keep her gaze from eventually wandering to where Hunter stood. And why shouldn't she? Sure, Sloane might tease her. Her mom might get wind of it and try to play matchmaker. There were a lot worse things in life. She knew because she'd endured them. Other members of her family had gone through truly terrible ordeals. What was a bit of annoying teasing in comparison? She had to believe Sloane wouldn't go too far and say something directly to Hunter.

All thought of what her sister might say or do disappeared when she saw the expression change on Hunter's face. Gone was any hint of a smile, replaced by a pinched concern visible even from where she stood half the width of the gallery away. Before she even consciously made the decision, she headed straight toward him.

Hunter's heart ached as he watched the confusion pull at his mom's face.

"Of course it's him," she said as she looked at the photo of a cowboy on horseback silhouetted against a setting sun and a herd of cattle.

She had been doing so well, having a good time, and then the confusion and frustration made another unwelcome appearance as she examined one of Angel's photos. His mom was absolutely convinced that the man on the horse was Hunter's dad, despite the fact that not only had Angel never been to their ranch but his dad had been gone almost a decade.

"Are you all enjoying yourselves?" Angel asked as she suddenly appeared at his elbow.

The moment their gazes connected he could tell she'd deduced his mom was having a bad moment. He'd opened his mouth to ask for some sort of help when his mom spoke instead.

"This is Hunter's dad, isn't it?" She sounded so sure that he wished that she was right.

There was a momentary flicker of surprise on Angel's face before her expression softened. "I can see where you might think that. It does look a lot like him with the sun behind him, doesn't it? But it's actually my dad. I took that on his birthday last year. There's nothing he likes more than going for a ride across the ranch. I'm sure Mr. Millbrook was the same way."

The woman was a marvel, a saint, a goddess. He wanted to pull her into his arms and kiss her, and it wasn't entirely because of his attraction to her. As he glanced at his mom, it was evident that while the confusion wasn't totally gone she also was beginning to accept Angel's explanation.

"Oh, I was so sure." And just like that the confusion was replaced by a sadness that was so strong it was almost visible in and of itself.

"You know," Angel said, "in truth the photo is shot in such a way that it can be representative of whoever we want to imagine in that spot." She reached into the bin below the larger framed photo on the wall and pulled out an eight-by-ten matted print. "You can put this up and imagine Mr. Millbrook out for an evening ride."

Hunter really appreciated Angel's kindness toward his mom, the gentle way she interacted with her without treating her like a child or someone who was sick.

But he still wished she hadn't pulled out the print. He had no idea how much it was, and his funds were tight. Sure, it appeared she might be giving it as a gift, but that didn't feel right, either. This was how she made her living, and she had a child to support as a single parent. Even though she had plenty of family to help out, Julia was still her daughter.

But when he saw how his mom slowly ran her fingertips across the print, he knew she had to keep it. Even if she now knew it wasn't his dad, it didn't matter. The picture made her think of him, hopefully bringing back some fond memories and not just a sense of loss, and he wasn't going to take that away from her.

His mom looked up at Angel with the shine of unshed tears in her eyes. "Thank you, hon. You have a kind heart."

"You're very welcome. I'm happy you like it. And it's the least I can do since Hunter worked so hard to make sure the gallery was all spiffed up for my opening."

His mom's gaze shifted to him, and she smiled with a mother's pride that had made him fidget when he was a kid. Now he couldn't get enough of it. He felt an urgent need to store up all the familiar expressions, all the pats on the back, all his mom's laughter and teasing so he'd never forget how they felt when she was gone. A lump formed in his throat at that thought, enough that he had to attempt to clear it.

"He's a good son, the best," she said.

Damn, was she trying to make him cry in public? The pressing need to flee the building almost overwhelmed him.

Mildred walked up then, and his mom turned to show her the print.

"Thank you for being so kind to her," Hunter said quietly so his mom wouldn't hear.

"Nothing to thank me for."

"I disagree."

She looked up at him, her dark eyes so beautiful he was momentarily speechless. Could he ask her out? Should he when it felt dangerous and irresponsible to leave his mom at home while he went and had a good time? He was searching for the right words when Merline drew Angel's attention.

"You're not going to have to haul the big frame back home," Merline said with a smile.

"Really?" Angel sounded stunned.

"Really. The buyers would like to meet you."

"Okay." Angel turned toward him. "Sorry, I need—"

"Go ahead. I should get Mom home anyway."

"Oh, okay. Thank you for coming." For a moment, she almost seemed hesitant to leave, but then she was being escorted through the crowd toward someone who had the disposable income necessary to buy the most expensive item on display. He watched her as she paused for a moment to speak to one of the gallery workers before he turned to tell his mom he'd be back in a minute. She was still smiling at the print in her hands.

Leaving his mom temporarily with Mildred, he walked over to the cash register where a young woman he didn't know was stationed. But when he pulled out his wallet, she shook her head.

"You don't owe anything, sir."

How could she possibly know what Angel had done? When he glanced in Angel's direction, she gave him a smile that said she had anticipated his trying to pay for the print. Though he didn't like feeling like a charity case, he smiled back. Not only was the woman beautiful, kind and talented, she was also smart enough to think three steps ahead of him.

Yeah, he needed to leave not just for his mother's sake. If he didn't get out of the gallery soon, he was going to be tempted to walk right up to Angel and kiss her like he'd never kissed anyone in his life. Once he had his mom safely home, then he could consider his next step regarding Angel Hartley.

Chapter 5

Angel sat at the kitchen table, enjoying the quiet of a house asleep. The only sounds came from the ticking clock in the kitchen and the hum of the refrigerator. It was peaceful after the constant talking during the exhibit opening. Not that she was complaining because the night had been a bigger success than she could have hoped. In addition to making a contact at one of the premier Western magazines and selling her biggest piece, she'd also sold three other framed photographs and a good number of matted prints. And the couple from Austin had ordered a larger version of her photograph depicting the most recent roundup at her family's ranch.

Yet even with all those successful aspects of the evening, the thing that she kept thinking about was Hunter and his mom. When she'd heard that Mrs. Millbrook had truly thought the photo of Angel's dad had instead been her late husband, it had almost broken Angel's heart. Especially when she'd seen the look on Hunter's face, like he was witnessing another piece of his mom slip away. She couldn't imagine what he was going through.

"What are you doing up, hon?"

Angel jumped at the sound of her mom's voice, making her realize how deeply she'd fallen into her thoughts.

"I didn't mean to startle you. I came in because I thought the light had just been left on."

"Wasn't sleepy yet."

"Still too excited about your big night?"

"Yeah. It went much better than I anticipated."

Her mom slipped into the chair opposite her. "I wasn't the least bit surprised. You take photos as if you were born with a camera in your hands."

"You're my mom. You have to say that."

"No, I have to love you and praise your kindergarten drawings. You're an adult now and I'll always tell you the truth. And that truth is I'm in awe of what you capture in your photos. I can be looking at the same thing you are through your lens, but somehow you seem to capture things I can't even see with my own eyes."

Angel's heart filled with her mother's praise. "That's the best compliment anyone has ever given me."

"Well, you just remember that if you ever doubt yourself."

Angel reached across the table and placed her hand atop her mom's. "I won the lottery when you and Dad adopted me."

"Then there are two lottery winners at this table because I got lucky five times over." Her mom smiled, then stood. "How about some of Lauren's leftover treats?"

"It's after midnight."

"And your point?"

Angel chuckled. "Sure, why not."

Her mom returned with a plate of assorted miniature desserts, and Angel's hand went immediately to one of the chocolate-orange treats. With the first bite, her thoughts drifted back to Hunter.

"Something else is on your mind," her mom said before taking a bite of a mini key lime pie.

Angel didn't deny it because her mom was just too good at reading her children. Instead, she told her about the interaction with Hunter's mom.

"That has to be the cruelest diagnosis in the world," her mom said.

"It just seems so unfair, especially since Hunter lost his father at a young age. Now to face losing his mom and being left alone. I hate how good people get such a raw deal sometimes."

"Life is, unfortunately, really unfair. We just have to remember to focus on the good things, to live life to its fullest while we can."

Angel watched her mom, searching for some extra meaning in her words. She didn't think Sloane had said anything to her about Hunter, but she couldn't be sure. Maybe she had and her mom was just tiptoeing into the topic.

"What?"

Angel shook her head. "Sometimes it feels like the things you say have two meanings."

"What other meaning could I possibly have? Perhaps that you like Hunter Millbrook?"

Angel sighed. "If Sloane still lived here, I'd be tempted to go duct-tape her mouth."

Her mom smiled. "Honey, your sister didn't say anything. She didn't have to. I saw how you looked his direction several times tonight."

Angel dropped her forehead into her hands. "I guess I'm not winning any awards for subtlety, huh?"

"I doubt anyone else noticed, except maybe your sister if she already suspected. I didn't even realize you and Hunter knew each other very well."

"We don't, not really. We just talked a little while he was doing some work around the gallery for Merline."

"But you'd like to get to know him better?"

"I don't know. Maybe." Yes, but something inside her made her scared to say it out loud. And her past, her role as Julia's protector, made her believe her answer should actually be a definitive no.

"I understand you were hurt badly when Dave left, but your life is far from over. And you deserve another chance to love someone and have him love you back."

"It just seems…scary, and possibly dangerous."

Her mother's face showed confusion. "You think Hunter is dangerous?"

Angel shook her head. "No, not like that. It's just… I've not had the best luck in the dating department. And I have to consider Julia as my number one priority in anything I do."

Not to mention that she wasn't sure if she could face any more rejection. Feeling as if your heart had taken a literal beating wasn't exactly what she called fun.

"Like you, I don't know Hunter well, but he seems like a good man. It was obvious tonight how much he cares about his mother."

"He does." The truth was he seemed like an all around great guy.

"But the prospect of dating again is still scary."

She nodded. "Not to mention that we won't be crossing paths as much anymore now that the exhibit opening is over."

"You could call him and ask him out to dinner, maybe go to a movie. Women make the first moves now, you know." Her mom grinned with a hint of the same matchmaking mischief she'd seen when her brothers and sisters had been the target.

"I don't know. I worry about Julia getting attached to someone only to get hurt when it doesn't work out. At least she never knew her dad."

"You're getting a little ahead of yourself, aren't you? We're just talking about a single date."

Her mom was right. Could she muster up the courage to do the asking? What if he said no?

She wasn't going to know until she tried, was she? Yes, Julia was the most important person in her life, but there was no denying a specific kind of loneliness that she'd been feeling even more since all her siblings had moved out to be with their spouses.

"Just think about it, okay?" her mom said.

"I will."

Her mom stood and took the now-empty plate to the dishwasher.

"Mom, Sloane told me that you blame yourself for the situation with Dave. That absolutely was not your fault. It was mine for trusting the wrong person."

And what if she did it again?

"I'm your mother. I'm supposed to protect you."

"And sometimes we don't know people are jerks until they decide to show their true colors. That was Dave. No one saw it, so no more blaming yourself, okay?"

Her mom didn't look like she was totally convinced

she hadn't failed in her maternal duties, but she at least nodded.

"I'm headed back to bed. Try to get some sleep."

"I will. Good night, Mom."

She did try, but the racing of her thoughts refused to let her rest for more than a couple of hours. She relived that awful moment when she'd told Dave she was pregnant only to hear him respond that it wasn't his problem, that she could keep the baby if she wanted but he had no intention of being a father. And the look he'd given her, as if he believed she'd gotten pregnant on purpose. Every time she thought about that expression on his face, she ground her teeth.

He hadn't lied, however, about his intent. Not only had he left Blue Falls, but the last she heard he was living somewhere in Mexico. After she'd managed to get past the initial pain, she'd gotten angry and determined that she would give her child a wonderful life with no help from him. Sometimes she was saddened by the fact that Julia was growing up without a father, but Angel did her best to fill both parental roles.

When her mind exhausted itself reliving those heart-breaking days and the fear she'd gone through at the thought of facing motherhood alone, she'd finally fallen asleep. But a mere two hours passed before she woke near dawn and her mind started swirling again, this time coming up with pros and cons for asking Hunter out to dinner. What if he wasn't interested in her? Yes, he'd been nice during all their interactions, but maybe he was like that with everyone. She wondered if he was one of those guys who'd be uncomfortable with the woman doing the asking. But most of all she worried that getting involved with him would be a mistake, one that could potentially hurt her daughter's tender heart, as well.

But then she thought about Lauren and what she'd been through with her ex-fiancé. Lauren had gone through hell, had been understandably wary of trusting another man, particularly when she had twin daughters to consider, and yet she'd found it in her heart to take a chance with Adam. Angel had never seen her brother so happy, and Lauren now had the perfect life. If Lauren could take that leap of faith, surely Angel could.

Still, as she went through her day, her thoughts fixated on whether to call Hunter and, if she did, what exactly she'd say. As she framed new photos to replace the ones that had sold at the gallery, she considered when would be the best time to call him. Of course, she'd have to find out his phone number first. Did he still have a house phone? She tried to quiet her riotous thoughts by playing Frisbee with Julia and Brent, but it was only a partial and temporary fix. By the time late afternoon rolled around, she decided to just call and get it over with. After finding a home phone number for the Millbrooks, she closed the door to her room, took a deep breath and dialed.

The phone rang four times before someone picked up, and Angel suddenly thought she might pass out. Seriously, she hadn't been this nervous about talking to a guy in her entire life. She needed to snap out of it.

"Hello?"

Was it her imagination or did he sound every bit as tired as she felt? For a fleeting moment, she imagined he'd lain awake thinking about her last night at the same time she was about him. Oh, good grief, now she was thinking in romantic movie scenarios.

"Oh, hey, Hunter."

There was silence on the other end of the line for a long moment before he replied, "Angel?"

"Yeah, how's it going?"

How's it going? Make that a romantic movie with an awkward teenage girl protagonist.

"Okay, you?"

"Fine." *Just do it, you goob.* "Listen, I was wondering if you'd like to go out to dinner."

Had she asked that as fast as it had seemed, as if it was all one word?

Again with the pause. "I'd really like that." Another pause while it sounded as if he walked away from wherever he'd been standing. "But I'm afraid to leave Mom by herself."

Angel's hope fell out from under her, but she couldn't be upset. She knew this wasn't a brush-off because she could hear the sadness in his voice. How could she help alleviate it?

"How about you and your mom come over for dinner with my family? Mom makes a killer chocolate cake."

"You don't have to do that."

"I know, but it'll be nice. Mom loves nothing more than cooking for people. And the house is a lot emptier than it used to be."

"I don't want to impose."

"Hunter, it's not imposing if someone invites you."

She caught the slightest hint of a laugh. "Okay, that sounds nice. What night works for you?"

"How about you talk to your mom and let me know? We're flexible."

"Sounds good."

Yeah, it did. It wasn't the date she imagined, but this was probably better, less awkward and risky.

Also much less chance of a good-night kiss.

She shook her head. Her mom was right. She was getting way ahead of herself instead of focusing on the fact that she'd see Hunter again. The thought made her giddy.

Hunter stood in the laundry room staring at the phone in his hand. All the time he'd spent imagining ways to ask Angel out and she ended up being the one doing the asking. Not that he minded if it led to the same result.

Well, not that he and his mom going to the Hartleys' house for dinner was a date, but at least he'd be able to see and talk to Angel. Maybe between now and then he could figure out a way to keep his mom safe so he could ask Angel out on a real date. Guilt gnawed at his middle. He hated it any time his mind even hinted at thinking his mom was a burden. She wasn't. Her condition was just a fact of life they had to deal with now.

"Who was on the phone?" his mom called from the living room where she'd been watching TV.

He walked back to the doorway between the kitchen and living room. "Angel Hartley. She just invited us over for dinner with her family."

For a moment, she looked confused and his heart sank. Had she forgotten who Angel was? But then she smiled, and there was a mischief in that smile that surprised him.

"That right? You sure I was part of that invitation?"

"Yes. Why wouldn't you be?" He wasn't going to tell her that the family dinner had been the second option Angel had given. She'd likely feel guilty, and that was the last thing he wanted her to feel. How many times had she given up something she might have wanted to do so that he could have fun instead?

"Just seems to me I'm not the one she wants to see again."

A thrill went through him that maybe the time had come when he could do more than imagine being with Angel. Sure, his life wasn't carefree. There were obstacles, but what relationship didn't have those?

"She said her mom really likes cooking for people and she has fewer to cook for now that all of Angel's brothers and her sister are married and in their own homes."

His mom searched his face, probably trying to figure out if he was bending the truth. He held up his hand. "Scout's honor. You can call and ask her yourself if you like."

She waved away that thought. "No need." She was quiet for a moment. "Is this because of what happened last night at the gallery? I don't want people feeling sorry for me, feeling like I have to be coddled."

Hunter crossed the living room and sank onto the ottoman in front of her chair.

"Mom, listen. I don't have any reason to doubt the sincerity of what Angel said, but you're also going to have to accept that people are going to feel sorry for you. It's human nature. Remember how you felt sorry for Mildred when Shawn was in the hospital? You wished you could help make it so that Mildred didn't have to go through all the pain and worry. That's how people feel when they hear someone, especially a good person like you, gets an unfair diagnosis. They can't help it."

She let out a long sigh. "I know, but it doesn't make it any easier. This isn't who I am," she said, motioning toward her head, where the disease was progressing.

He took her hands in his. "I know. Everyone knows. But don't you think that you should live every moment you have to the fullest and go to dinner when someone invites you?"

She locked gazes with him. "Your father would be so proud of you. We couldn't have raised a better son."

That damn lump made a return appearance in his throat, and he felt desperate to lighten the moment. "You're right about that."

As he'd hoped, his mom laughed. "Okay, I'll go, even though I still think this was just a ruse so she could see you again."

Fearing his mom might be able to see the heat rising up his neck into this face, he stood. Instinct was to deny what she'd said, but he found he couldn't. Not when Angel had called to ask him out on a date. He managed to keep his smile hidden until he made it to the bathroom. As he took off his clothes coated with another long day of ranch work, the smile continued to grow until he was pretty sure it could light up the bathroom like the midday sun.

Maybe tonight was the beginning of his life taking a turn for the better.

It was times like this when Angel wished she had Lauren's talent in the kitchen. Or her mom's easy way of putting together what seemed like effortless but delicious meals. Even though she knew her mom didn't mind the extra work of preparing food for two additional people, it didn't feel right since it had been Angel's idea to invite Hunter and his mom to dinner.

So Angel did what she could until her mom ushered her out of the kitchen to go pick up Julia from the school bus. It was a big day not only for Angel but also for her daughter since today marked the end of the school year and the beginning of summer vacation.

But instead of the big smile and boundless excitement Angel expected to see, the moment Julia stepped off the bus it was obvious she'd been crying.

Angel's stomach sank. Julia wasn't much of a crier after she reached her toddler years. Something was very wrong for her to look red-eyed and upset. Angel hurried toward her daughter and dropped to one knee in front of her.

"Sweetie, what's wrong? Are you hurt? Sick?"

Julia shook her head as her eyes began to shine even more.

"Did your real mom throw you in the trash?"

Angel nearly fell over backward as if she'd taken a physical blow.

"Why would you say that?"

"Cara said your mom didn't want you, so she threw you in the trash. That I'm trash, too, because all Indians are trash."

Angel experienced a surge of rage like she'd never had in her life. She wanted to throttle Cara's parents because she knew that was where their daughter had learned that racist viewpoint. Not for the first time, she wished teaching children to be racist bigots was a crime. But she couldn't let Julia see the anger seething inside her. Julia's childhood innocence had already taken a hit today. But she knew the time to tell Julia the full truth had finally come.

"Cara is wrong. We are not trash. That's just a mean thing some people say to feel better about themselves." Angel was no stranger to the occasional racist remark

herself—either because she was Native or some igno-
rant fool lumped her in with her Hispanic classmates as
if that was a bad thing.

"How about we grab some of Grandma's cookies and
go for a walk? It's such a pretty day and you're officially
on summer vacation!"

Julia's face brightened a little, but it was obvious
this was something that had really wounded her. Angel
pulled Julia into her arms and put all her love into the
hug before escorting her back to the truck.

As she drove back to the house, it took all her will-
power to appear calm when what she really wanted to
do was go give Cara Dalton's parents a very large piece
of her mind. Maybe even a kick to Danny Dalton's man
parts if she was being honest. But Julia's feelings were
a million times more important than her own at the moment.

When they reached the house, Angel went to the
kitchen to get some cookies while Julia dropped off her
backpack in her room. Angel's mom looked up from
where she was frosting her famous chocolate cake, and
immediately concern transformed her expression.

"What's wrong?"

"Today's the day."

Her mom looked momentarily confused before realization clicked. "Someone said something?"

Angel nodded. "Danny Dalton's girl." She didn't say
anything else because her mom knew exactly what kind
of person Danny was. She'd been forced into a come-to-
Jesus meeting with his parents when he'd said some truly
awful things to Angel when they were kids. Racism, unfortunately, sometimes got passed from one generation of

a family to the next. Her mom looked ready to do battle again, so much so that Angel gave her a big hug.

Her mom patted her on the back. "You've got this. And Julia is a strong, smart girl. She'll understand."

As anxiety gripped her middle, Angel truly hoped her mom was right about that. She'd thought maybe she'd have a bit more time before she had to divulge what had happened to her, how she'd come to be a Hartley in the first place, but perhaps it was better to get this conversation over with before Julia got any older. It'd be worse if Julia reached an age where she could harbor resentment toward her mother for keeping the truth from her.

Their walk didn't take them very far. With the way Julia was looking down at her feet as she walked, she wasn't seeing any of their surroundings anyway. Best to get this conversation over with.

"Here, let's sit and have some cookies." Angel indicated one of the picnic tables beneath the shade trees.

When Julia only picked at a cookie she normally would have devoured, Angel took a deep breath and dived in.

"I've always told you that I—like your aunt and uncles—am adopted, but I haven't told you the whole story. I want to tell you now so that you'll know the truth if anyone ever says anything mean to you again, okay?"

Julia nodded, making eye contact with Angel for the first time since they left the bus stop.

How she wished she didn't have to tell her daughter about the reality of who her birth grandmother was.

"Unlike my brothers and sister, I didn't ever live with my birth family. I don't even know who they are or where they're from. My birth mother left me at a hospital with only a note saying that my name was Angel and she couldn't take care of me. Your grandparents took me in straight from the hospital."

"So your real mom didn't throw you in the trash but she did give you away?"

"Yes. Sometimes it's for the best. They do it so that their baby can have a better life."

"Then she loved you?" Julia's forehead scrunched as she obviously tried to understand how a mother could love her baby but give her away.

"I'm sure she did." Actually, she wasn't sure of any such thing. The note left with her at the hospital could have been a lie, something to cover up a crime or that her birth mother really just didn't want her.

But that was a bit too much harsh truth for a child Julia's age.

"Do you think she thinks about you?"

How many times had Angel wondered that same thing? "I don't know, sweetie. Maybe."

The truth was Angel had no idea if the woman was even still alive. Despite having a wonderful family, Angel couldn't help feeling a certain rootlessness sometimes, as if she had one foot in some mystery world she couldn't identify. If nothing else, she'd like to know her heritage, what tribal connections she had. She wanted that knowledge—for herself and Julia—but she'd also always been afraid to pursue it. What if she didn't like what she found? If she did by some miracle find her birth mother, it was possible she'd also find out the woman had never cared for her at all. And what if she was the kind of person Angel wanted nowhere near Julia? Maybe some things were best left unknown.

Julia still had a puzzled look on her face.

"Do you have more questions?"

"Why did Cara say Indians are trash?"

Angel pushed down her anger again and spent several minutes trying to explain racism to a first grader.

"That's dumb," Julia said when Angel told her some people believed that white people were better than those who had different-colored skin.

Angel smiled. "I agree. It is dumb." She had stronger words for it than that, but *dumb* would suffice in the presence of her child.

She watched as Julia took another bite of her cookie. She'd swear she could hear the gears turning in Julia's head.

"How exactly did the topic of race come up with Cara anyway?" After all, Julia had never said anything about the girl giving her trouble before.

"Mrs. Hanson said next year our teachers will have us do family trees, so we might want to start working on them over the summer."

But how did Cara know the story about Angel being abandoned? Had her father told Cara the story for some reason? If so, he was even more despicable than she remembered.

"Cara said I'll fail the assignment since I don't know who my family is."

"But you do know. I'm your family. And your grandparents, aunts, uncles, cousins. Family means lots of different things, and you are a Hartley. Don't ever believe anyone if they say you're not."

"But we don't look like everyone else."

"No, we don't, but you're every bit as beautiful as your blonde aunt or your curly-haired uncle."

Julia giggled. "I'm going to tell Uncle Adam you said he's beautiful."

Angel's heart lifted, thankful to see a smile on Julia's face again.

"You know, I bet Aunt Lauren will back me up on that one."

They sat and ate the rest of their cookies. Angel was aware that the appointed time for Hunter and his mom to arrive for dinner was getting closer, but she wasn't about to rush Julia in case she had more questions.

"Do you wish we looked like everyone else?" Julia asked.

"No. We're special just the way we are." Although there had been times when she'd thought maybe life would be easier if she did look like her parents. Maybe then she wouldn't wonder so much about where she came from. She'd probably still wonder about her birth parents, but it wouldn't be the same. She didn't think she'd also always wonder about her cultural identity.

"Do you think your mom who gave you away would like me?"

"Of course, sweetie. What's not to like? She would count herself lucky to have such a kind, smart, beautiful granddaughter." Angel hoped that was truth, and for a moment she wished she could give that to Julia. But then she remembered that her parents, the ones who counted, loved Julia enough for a dozen grandparents.

They sat for a few more minutes, but Julia finally ran out of questions.

"Okay, we need to go back to the house. We're having company for dinner tonight."

"Who?"

"Hunter Millbrook and his mom. They came to the art exhibit opening the other night."

"Is she the lady who got confused?"

Angel hadn't realized that Julia knew about that. "Yes, but don't mention it."

"Okay. Is it because she's old? Amber says her grandpa gets lost sometimes."

"Partly. She has a disease that makes her forget things, but not all the time. But we don't want to mention it and make her feel bad."

Julia nodded. "Got it." And then she made the motion of zipping her lips and throwing the key over her shoulder.

As they walked back to the house, hand in hand, Angel prayed that Julia never had to watch her slowly lose her memories and grasp the present. She couldn't imagine a worse fate for a child, and her heart broke once again for the future that lay in front of Hunter and his mom.

Chapter 6

It wasn't Angel who greeted Hunter and his mom at the front door to the Hartley house but rather her sister, Sloane, wearing a smile so wide one would think she'd just won the title of Miss America.

"Welcome," she said and held the door open wide for them to step inside.

Angel entered the living room from a hallway off to the right, looking a little frazzled if he had to name her expression. A smile tugged at the edges of his mouth at the thought that having him here in her home unnerved her in a good way.

After a brief smile shot his way, she shifted her gaze to her sister. "I didn't know you were going to be here tonight."

There was no mistaking a bit of suspicion in her voice.

"We heard Mom was making chocolate cake, so we couldn't pass that up."

"We?"

As if to visually answer Angel's question, Ben Hartley and his wife, Mandy, as well as a man who must be Sloane's husband came into the living room from what looked to be a combination kitchen and dining area.

Angel seemed to shake off whatever annoyance had been there a moment before and set about making introductions. When she shook his mom's hand, she said, "I'm so glad you could make it. You're honestly making Mom's night."

"That's true," her mom said. "I'm happiest when cooking for a lot of people."

Mrs. Hartley escorted his mom into the kitchen, and everyone else moved away from the entrance so that he could finally step closer to Angel.

"Either your mom's chocolate cake is legendary, or your family is really interested in the fact you invited us for dinner."

"Actually, it's both. Mom could ensure the signing of peace treaties with the promise of her chocolate cake. But the moratorium on meddling in the love life of the baby of the family is evidently over."

He wanted to ask why there had been a moratorium, but then he thought better of it. Maybe they'd been hands-off because of the breakup with Julia's father.

"I'm sorry to put you in this situation," she said.

"Don't worry about it. I'm not."

She smiled at him again, and he'd swear the temperature of the room went up several degrees.

Once they were all seated at the table and passing around bowls and platters filled with food that smelled delicious, he caught Sloane's gaze on him and she smiled with undisguised mischief.

"So, how did you like Angel's exhibit opening the other night?" she asked.

"We enjoyed it. Right, Mom?"

"Very much. Your sister is very talented."

"Thank you," Angel said.

Hunter was pretty sure she punched her sister under the table, causing him to have to hide laughter that wanted to bubble up and out of him.

"Are you a photographer, too?" Julia asked from her seat next to her mother.

He smiled at her. "No, afraid not. I have a small ranch."

"Oh, like us!"

"Yes, though not as big."

"Do you have lots of brothers and sisters like Mom?"

He shook his head. "No, I'm an only child."

"Me, too. But I have cousins now. Do you have cousins?"

"A couple. They don't live in Blue Falls, though."

"I'm sorry."

"It's okay." What a sweet kid.

"That's enough interrogation," Angel said to her daughter. "Eat your dinner or no chocolate cake."

There was a gentleness to the direction, and he caught Angel watching Julia throughout the meal as if she was concerned about her. Was she afraid she'd ask something embarrassing? A sudden thought formed that maybe she was regretting having asked him out on a date, which had led to this larger family gathering.

His mom's laughter drew his attention, and he listened for a few minutes while his mom and Mrs. Hartley shared funny stories from their kids' childhoods. He didn't even object when his mom pulled out the one about how she'd caught him sleepwalking in the front yard buck naked when he was four. It was too good to see her really enjoying herself.

He glanced across the table to find Angel stifling a giggle of her own at the story.

"I guess it's a good thing we didn't have neighbors," he said.

"Or that you weren't older when it happened," Sloane said.

Angel didn't even try to hide the slap of her sister's arm. Sloane just laughed in response.

Hunter soaked it all up, not able to remember when there had last been this much laughter around his family's dinner table. He wanted it to go on all night, sleep be damned.

When Mrs. Hartley served dessert and he took his first bite, he realized Angel hadn't been lying. It was literally the best chocolate cake he'd ever tasted.

"This is delicious," his mom said before he could.

No matter the topic of conversation—be it ranching, rodeo or what Julia and her cousin Brent planned to do over their summer vacations—his mom seemed engaged. She did forget a couple of things she should have remembered, but on the whole it wasn't too bad. When they moved to the living room, she surprised him by even getting down on the floor to color with Julia. The sight of the two of them together caused such a large lump to form in his throat that he had to step outside to get some fresh air. He'd go back in soon, not wanting to leave her for too long, but he needed a few minutes alone.

The sun had fallen below the horizon, painting the sky in streaks of orange, pink and purple. He made his way off the porch and walked farther along the drive past the barn. He spotted some picnic tables and went to sit atop one to watch the changes in the western sky. That was where Angel found him a few minutes later.

"You okay?" she asked as she joined him atop the table.

"Yeah, fine."

"You forget I'm a mom. I know a fib when I hear one."

He looked down at his hands loosely clasped between his knees. "When I saw Mom coloring with Julia, it hit me right in the chest. For the first time I realized she might never get to enjoy being a grandmother." He realized how that might sound to her and met her gaze. "I don't mean—"

Angel held up a hand to stop his bumbling explanation.

"I know you're not trying to guilt me into a quickie marriage." She smiled, amused by the idea, then sobered. "I'm sorry you're going through this. I can't imagine."

"Not gonna lie. It sucks."

Angel reached over and entwined her hand with his. While he'd imagined touching her countless times, now that it was finally happening he was overcome by so many emotions—and, quite honestly, fatigue—that he took a shaky breath.

"Do you mind if I give you a bit of unsolicited advice?" she asked.

"No."

"It's admirable how you take care of your mom, but you need take care of yourself, as well. Otherwise, you risk running yourself in the ground."

"Easier said than done. There never seems to be enough hours in the day." And, unfortunately, he didn't have any brothers or sisters to share the load. "Though this was nice tonight. Thank you for inviting us to dinner. Between this and the exhibit opening, it gives me hope that Mom will be less hesitant to leave home."

"Good. I'm glad."

"I'm sorry I had to decline going out, just the two of us. I wanted to."

"Really?"

He turned more toward her, wondering if she thought he'd used not being able to leave his mom as an excuse to brush her off. Her hand still in his, he said, "Yes. I'm going to be honest here. I've had a crush on you for a long time." Angel's eyes widened so much that he couldn't help but laugh. "You look surprised."

"Well, I am. That's not something you hear every day. For how long?"

"I'm afraid if I tell you, you'll think I'm pathetic."

"Never."

He examined her eyes, saw nothing but truth there. Part of him wondered if this was just another of his many dreams about her.

"Since your freshman year."

"No," she said in obvious disbelief.

He nodded. "Yes."

"Why didn't you ever say something?"

"Never seemed like the right time."

Angel tilted her head slightly. "Not ever in the past ten years?"

"See, pathetic."

"No, but I am curious. I'd ask if this was about Dave, but he's not always been part of the picture."

Oh, hell. Why not tell her? He'd already hopped aboard the embarrassment train. Might as well stay on for the entire journey.

Feeling like a fool, he enumerated all the various obstacles to asking her out stretching from their differences in age during high school to his present concerns about his mom.

"Well, I can think of two of those reasons I could have done without, although because of Dave I have Julia. Going through that breakup was worth it just to have her."

"She seems like a great kid."

"She is. I'm very lucky in that regard."

"Are you worried about her?"

The question obviously surprised Angel. "Why do you ask?"

"You kept watching her at dinner, like you were concerned about something."

Angel's hand slipped out of his as she turned to face the darkening pasture dotted by part of the Hartleys' herd. "She was upset when she got off the bus today." She told him everything Julia's classmate had said. "What's sad is that it's not really a surprise. Cara's dad is a bigot of the first order."

Hunter's hands clenched into fists. "Are you going to confront the parents?"

"I haven't decided the best course of action yet."

"If you do, don't go alone. I'll go with you."

She looked over at him. "Thank you. That means a lot. But I've got quite the intimidating posse at my beck and call. Julia's uncles and aunt would be more than happy to make sure she never has to go through anything like that again."

Of course she had plenty of backup if she needed it, but it didn't lessen his desire to be at her side if she faced off against the man who was teaching his daughter to hate other kids just because their skin was a different color.

"Have you faced it, too?" He hoped the subject wasn't too personal.

She nodded. "Sometimes, though not anywhere near as much as lots of people do. I don't know for sure, but I think it might be worse for Native Americans who live where they actually have larger populations, such as in the communities around reservations."

"I've never understood some people's need to hate others just because they're different in some way. Be damned boring if we were all the same."

"I wish more people had that attitude."

"Maybe they will in time."

"Maybe, but it breaks my heart and makes me angry all at the same time when I see new generations being taught the same bigotry. Sometimes I think it's a miracle that I got adopted right after I was born. I could have easily spent my entire childhood in a group home or foster care."

"So…you never knew your birth parents?"

"Nope." Angel picked at her cuticles.

"I'm sorry. That was too personal."

"It's okay. It's not a big secret, really. I was left at a hospital in Austin with a note with my name and that I needed a good home. And that's the extent of my knowledge about where I come from."

"You couldn't find out more?"

"I haven't tried." She shrugged. "I've thought about it, but I always worried that I'd be disappointed in some way. Either I wouldn't find out anything at all, or I wouldn't like what I did find. Although now I wonder if that was a mistake. What prompted this whole thing at school today was the teacher mentioning that the kids would have to do a family tree next year. I mean, Julia can just do the Hartley family tree and it will suffice. But am I robbing her of her true heritage, what's in her blood, if I don't try to find out?"

"That's not for me to answer."

She shook her head, then looked up at the sky and the last bit of light giving way to the first stars. "On the other hand, I worry about exposing her to something that could hurt her even more."

He wondered if it was more than that, if she feared she might get hurt as well as Julia. It already had to be difficult knowing that she'd been abandoned, no matter if her birth mother had the best of intentions.

"There have been times when I wished my birth mom would find me, take the decision out of my hands so I didn't have to make it." She made a swirling motion with her fingers next to her temple. "I get in this endless debate with myself—should I or shouldn't I look for her?"

"I can see how that would seem easier."

It hit him anew just how much he liked her, how much he wanted to spend time with her. Could he ask Mildred or one of his mom's other friends to visit with his mom for an evening so he could take Angel out on a proper date?

"Would you go out with me if you knew it might be a while before I could arrange a second date? If you enjoyed the first one enough to agree to a second one, that is."

At the shift in the topic of conversation, she exchanged her stargazing for looking at him again. "Why don't you ask me and we'll find out?"

"Angel Hartley, will you go out to dinner with me? I can't promise anything fancy, or—"

"Yes."

He smiled. "I wasn't quite finished."

"You asked the important part."

He fought the urge to kiss her because despite his attraction, it didn't feel like the right time. Not on the heels of the heavy topics they'd found themselves discussing. Hopefully the right time would come.

"Well, I better get Mom home before she gets too tired."

As they stood, Angel surprised him by squeezing his hand and planting a quick peck on his cheek. "You're a good son. Your mom is lucky to have you."

He wanted to thank her, but the words couldn't force their way past the well of emotion. And she seemed to understand because she smiled and turned back toward the house. After he managed a deep breath, he fell into step beside her.

Later, after he was home and his mom had gone to bed, he sat on the front steps of the house where he grew up and let the events of the night replay in his mind. The ranch that stretched out into the darkness might be more modest than the Hartleys' Rocking Horse Ranch, and he would have loved to have his father for longer. But he counted himself very lucky. He at least knew his parents and was loved by them. He couldn't imagine what it must be like to not have a clue about the identity of your real parents or any idea where you came from. To want the truth but be scared to search for it.

He understood her concerns about seeking out her birth parents, and he wondered what he'd do in the same situation. He had a feeling the need to know would win out. What if there was a way to find out for her? Would she see that as an invasion of her privacy? A little general research wouldn't hurt anyone, though.

So he spent the next several minutes doing web searches about tracking down birth parents and stories of babies abandoned at hospitals. He was stunned to even find a brief story about Angel being abandoned. It didn't reveal anything other than what she'd told him, except the fact that her birthday was coming up soon. The article didn't reveal the exact day, but he had a window based on the date on the article.

After he stopped reading, he opened up a text window. He considered texting Angel, but thought better of it. This was something better discussed in person, if at all. Instead, he pulled up the contact for Pete Kayne, a friend of his who was now with the Texas Highway Patrol, and asked him a general question about how he'd start looking for someone's birth parents if they didn't know their names or where they were from. He was surprised by how quickly he got a reply.

Why are you asking?

Asking for a friend. Really.

Let me do some checking. Will get back to you.

Hunter thanked him, then set his phone aside. Just as he looked up, he spotted a shooting star. There were so many things he could wish for, but the streak was gone from the sky before he could settle on one. Not that it mattered. It was his experience that more came from hard work and trying to be a good person than wishes.

Despite that, it didn't keep him from wishing to have a lot more years with his mom, that her truly bad time with the disease would be short-lived. Yes, he wanted her to live a long time, but not as an empty shell that used to be his mother.

On a happier note, he wished for the wisdom to make all the right moves where Angel was involved. And he wished for her to find her birth family if that was what she wanted, and that what she found would add to her happiness rather than take away from it.

As he leaned back on his hands and looked up at the clear night sky, he also wished that soon he'd know what it was like to kiss Angel Hartley.

Chapter 7

Angel stepped into Gia's Pizza, keenly aware of how very out of practice she was at dating. There had been plenty of times over the past few years when she'd thought she might never chance a date again. But then something about a few interactions with Hunter made her willing to give it a try. He, at least, didn't seem to be the type to have any rude surprises up his sleeve. Of course, Dave hadn't, either, but she was older now and hopefully wiser.

Hunter smiled and rose quickly to his feet when he spotted her. She imagined him kissing her on the cheek as she had him—she still couldn't quite believe she'd done that—but he simply nodded toward the table where he'd been sitting.

"I got a booth, but we can move if you'd rather sit at a table with chairs."

"No, I actually prefer booths. More comfortable."

How odd to engage in such small talk after they'd discussed much deeper and important subjects a few nights before. Maybe that had been easier because they weren't really on a date then. She hoped making it official didn't lead to a night of awkwardness.

"Great. We're in agreement. Now to see if we can agree on the best kind of pizza."

"Well, unless you say pepperoni and pineapple, you'd be wrong."

"How did you know that was my favorite?" He feigned complete surprise at her amazing mind reading skills.

She laughed a little. "Seriously, what is your favorite?"

"I've never met any kind of pizza I didn't like."

"Well, you're a pretty agreeable date so far."

"I aim to please."

Oh, if he only knew what sort of images that simple response brought to mind. She looked down at the menu, hoping he wouldn't be able to read the truth in her eyes.

But when the waitress appeared beside their table, they went with pepperoni and pineapple and a side of mozzarella cheese sticks.

"So, how's your mom?" she asked.

"Good. She and some of her friends are playing cards tonight. And it was actually her idea. I hadn't said anything, but on the way home from your place the other night, she told me I needed to ask you out."

"Did you tell her you already had?"

"Yes, and I think she was a little annoyed because she didn't get to use the big speech to convince me that she had planned."

"Julia hasn't stopped talking about her. She loved that your mom got down on the floor and colored with her. She even asked if she could go over to your house and play with Evelyn." Angel smiled at the sweetness of her child's heart. "She's never had any problem making friends with people nowhere near her age."

"Mom would love that. You're welcome anytime."

"If she doesn't stop bringing it up, I might take you up on that."

"I'm serious. I think it'd be good for Mom, and if it makes Julia happy, all the better." He hesitated for a moment before continuing. "And I wouldn't mind if Julia's mom came along."

"Mind if Julia's mom brings her camera? Now that all the prep for the exhibit is over, I've been itching to get back out to take some new photos."

"You're welcome to, but I don't know if you'll find anything worth photographing."

"Leave that to me."

"Well, if there's something, I'm sure you'll find it."

She already knew one thing that would yield great photos, and he was sitting across from her.

"So, what's next after the exhibit?"

"I got some special orders from it, but probably the most exciting thing was I met someone who works at *West* magazine the night of the opening. It was sheer luck that he ended up there since he was vacationing nearby. I can't tell you how big of a deal it would be to get some of my photos into that magazine, but it's really hard. Only the most talented photographers even have a chance."

"Then you should have no problem."

"While I appreciate the compliment, there are lots of talented photographers and very few slots."

"Well, you won't know until you try, as they say."

"Yeah, I just hate getting my hopes up too high in case things don't pan out how I want."

Hunter averted his gaze in a way that seemed odd, but the sound of someone snorting in what seemed like disgust drew her attention to another table on the other side of the restaurant. And there sat Danny Dalton staring at her with undisguised distaste.

"What is it?" Hunter asked as he looked in the same direction.

"Nothing."

But Danny stood suddenly and crossed toward her, shoving chairs out of his way. Just great.

"I heard you went to the school to complain about my daughter."

Stay calm.

"I did."

"You should mind your own business."

"I'd be happy to if your daughter didn't spout racist things at my daughter."

"You—"

Hunter stood suddenly, inserting himself between where Danny loomed and Angel was doing her best to sit calmly as if he didn't bother her at all. Though she should take care of this herself, it gave her a surge of satisfaction that Hunter had a good four inches in height on Danny, forcing him to look up at Hunter.

"You're going to want to step away, all the way back to your table."

"This isn't any of your business."

"It is when you try to intimidate my date."

Danny made that sound of disgust again. "What, white girls not good enough for you?"

"Common decency not good enough for you?" Nothing Hunter said was a threat, but there was no denying the unspoken intent. Either Danny needed to retreat or he was going to regret it.

Danny looked past Hunter at Angel. "Keep your daughter away from mine."

Ice in her veins, she stared at him hard. "Ditto."

Danny turned and headed back toward where his wife and Cara sat. He muttered something that she couldn't make out but was no doubt unflattering. Hunter didn't move until Danny sank back into his own booth. Then he slowly sat down across from Angel right as their pizza arrived.

To be honest, her appetite had taken a hit.

"Would you like to take this somewhere else to eat?" Hunter asked.

She shook her head. "I'm not about to give him that satisfaction. What is that saying? Living well is the best revenge. I say eating well and pretending nothing happened is the best way to annoy a bigot."

He smiled and picked up a gooey slice of New York–style pizza. "Sounds like a good plan to me."

After they both took a few bites, he wiped his mouth with a napkin and said, "I hope you don't mind that I stepped in like that. I just don't condone men who act like that toward women."

"Normally, I like to fight my own battles, but it gave me a good bit of pleasure to see you owning that altercation."

"So you talked to the school about what happened, I take it."

"Yes. I spoke to the principal, who said she'd make sure the teachers next year knew about it. She also evidently followed through on calling Cara's parents."

As they ate, she did her best to ignore the Dalton family's stares in her direction. To his credit, Hunter did a good job of distracting her as they exchanged stories about growing up on ranches—the good, the bad and the downright hilarious. Despite a lot of similarities and a lot of positive stories from his youth, she detected a layer of sadness, too, one he might not even realize was there.

"You miss your dad, don't you?"

He glanced at her, probably surprised by the turn of conversation, but then nodded. "Every day. Never expected to lose him so soon. I guess when you're a teenager, you just don't think those types of thoughts."

"Did your parents not want more kids or was it not a choice?"

"Mom just never got pregnant again."

"I guess another of those things teenagers never think about is how lucky they are to have lots of siblings for when things get tough."

Hunter picked up a slice of pizza and just looked at it. "Yeah, I've thought a lot about how different life might be if I had a brother or sister. But some things aren't meant to be."

Movement from across the restaurant drew her attention, and she saw that the Daltons were leaving. Thank goodness. Maybe she could relax more without getting a hole stared into the side of her head. But while Danny and his wife, Rena, didn't look her way, Cara decided to get in one parting shot by sticking her tongue out at Angel.

Angel barely resisted the urge to respond in kind, but she had to be the responsible adult in this interaction. So instead, she smiled and waved at Cara before returning her attention to the pizza in front of her.

"I really hope she and Julia aren't in the same class next year."

"Can you request that?"

"Probably. I didn't think about it before. But I don't know if that would just be teaching Julia to avoid her problems instead of facing them head-on."

Hunter put the slice of pizza he'd been eating back on his plate and leaned against the booth. "Do you think it would help or hinder Julia if she actually knew her heritage?"

"I don't know. I mean, it's obvious the heritage is Native, which is the reason Cara was such a little snot to begin with."

"But you wouldn't be finding out for Cara's benefit or her family. You'd be finding out for you and Julia."

"I get the feeling you think I should pursue it."

"That's your decision. I just think that in your position, all the questions would drive me crazy."

She swirled the last of the cheese sticks in the marinara sauce but didn't take a bite. "It's not as easy a decision as it might seem. I'll have to think about it."

Sure, she'd thought about it plenty of times, but not too seriously. She wished she'd receive some sign that actually starting to search for her birth parents was the right choice, that it wouldn't lead to more heartache.

"Enough of all the serious talk," Hunter said. "This is supposed to be a date, not therapy, right?"

"Right." But when she tried to think of something fun and frivolous to talk about, she came up blank. When she looked across the table at Hunter, he seemed to be in the same boat. Something about that made her laugh. "We're a pitiful pair, aren't we?"

"I think this is what being out of practice dating looks like."

She laughed. "You're right about that."

"I hear the only way you get good at anything is lots of practice."

Her heart sped up at the thought of spending more time with him, even if they did have their awkward moments. "I'd be okay with that."

He smiled, then shifted his attention to the waitress who'd brought the check. After he handed over enough cash to pay for dinner, the waitress thanked him for the tip and walked back toward the register.

"You have a nice smile."

Hunter looked surprised at her comment. "Thanks. So do you. I've always thought so. To be honest, sometimes when I'd see you smile I'd nearly trip over my own feet."

"Oh, now you're just making up stuff."

"Nope. That's one hundred percent true."

She felt her cheeks heat and wondered if he could tell. "I don't know what to say."

"You don't have to say anything." He glanced at the front door when it opened, then back at her. "Do you have time for an ice-cream cone?"

"I do, although I don't know where I'll put it." She placed her hand on her stomach, which felt pretty full at the moment.

"Maybe we could take a walk around the lake first."

"That sounds nice."

Hunter was the picture of chivalry as he held the door open for her, as he adjusted his stride to match hers while they walked down the street and turned onto the sidewalk that led past all the shops on Main Street. A lot of them were closed now, with the exception of the eateries. When they reached the grassy area that surrounded the lake, Hunter held out his hand. With her stomach feeling fluttery, she placed her hand in his and allowed him to guide her toward the path that circled the lake.

Once they'd walked for a couple of minutes, she took a deep breath and looked out across the surface of Blue Falls Lake. The light from the lampposts along the path shone along the surface of the water.

"It's so peaceful out here at night," she said, "when it's not crowded with people."

"Yeah. You know, I can't remember the last time I actually walked around here."

"Me, neither. I'm always so busy, and when I'm in town it's for other reasons."

"Same. And every time I'm away from the ranch, I feel this need to hurry and get back." He slowed and looked over at her. "I didn't mean that I want to rush back right now."

"I know. But if you need to go, I'll understand." She would miss this feeling of connection and intimacy she hadn't experienced in a long time, but she'd understand.

"No. Mildred told me in no uncertain terms that if I got back too early, she wasn't going to let me in the house."

Angel laughed. "Well, that makes you wonder what they're getting up to, doesn't it? If this wasn't Blue Falls, I might think they'd ordered some male dancers for the evening."

"Ew. Please, I don't need the thought of my mom watching strippers in my head."

"Boom-chicka-wow-wow," she said in a singsong way.

"You're just evil."

She was still laughing when they reached the stairs leading up to the viewing platform near the waterfalls that gave the town its name. The sound of the water flowing into the lake relaxed her.

"I love that sound."

Hunter didn't respond but he seemed to be enjoying it, as well. She closed her eyes and inhaled deeply the damp, misty air. A rumble caused her to open her eyes in time to see a flash of lightning in the distance.

"Looks like we should head back," Hunter said as he pointed toward where she'd seen the lightning.

When they turned to retrace their steps, she hesitated long enough to look at Blue Falls lit up in the night. She didn't take many night photos, but she wished she had the equipment to capture the image.

Another rumble of thunder, closer this time, spurred her into action. They were only halfway back to Main Street when the wind kicked up suddenly at their backs. Hunter grasped her hand.

"This one's moving fast."

And in the next moment, they were running, hand in hand. When the first cold drops hit her back, immediately soaking through her thin cotton top, she squealed. The sky opened up right as they reached the grassy area that led back up to Main Street. By the time Hunter pulled her under the canopy in front of the furniture store, she was soaked. She wasn't the only one. Her breath caught when she saw how his shirt was plastered to his chest. Water dripped from his hair down over his face, and she reached up before she could think about what she was doing. She wiped some of the water from his cheek.

Hunter wrapped his hand around hers and held her gaze. "Why did you ask me out?"

She managed a smile. "I seem to remember you asking me out."

"You asked first."

"That's a technicality."

"But still the truth." He didn't let go of her hand but lowered it so that it rested against his wet chest.

Was he trying to short-circuit her neglected libido?

"I guess I just saw you in a different light." A neon one that screamed, *Look at how sexy this man is!*

"It was the brownie, wasn't it?" he said, teasing. "The power of chocolate."

"Well, that didn't hurt." Should she tell him the truth? Would it sound shallow? "Although if you hadn't looked so good in those jeans up on the gallery roof, the brownie likely wouldn't have been enough by itself."

The grin that formed on his face could only be described as rakish, a look she didn't think he wore very often.

"That right?"

"Don't go getting a big head over it. You know, now that I think about it, it was probably the sun. That's right. Baked all common sense right out of my head."

Whatever silly thing she'd been about to say next ceased to exist as Hunter's mouth dropped to hers. He pulled her close and she felt more clearly the firmness she'd seen outlined beneath his shirt. Her blood heated and rushed through her veins, heating the chill from the rain into nonexistence. The need to rip off clothing and get even closer to him hit her with such force that she moaned into his mouth, which resulted in his arms tightening around her back.

How could she have forgotten how good it felt to be held in a man's arms? To be kissed thoroughly?

Maybe because it had never felt like this with anyone else. Yes, it'd been a while, but she was pretty sure of that assessment as she clung to Hunter.

Thunder boomed so loudly right above their heads that they both jumped, ending the kiss. It felt like a celestial scolding for their very public display of affection. She laughed at that thought and dropped her forehead to Hunter's chest.

"The heavens seem to think we're getting carried away," she said.

As if to punctuate her words, the rain started coming down even harder.

"What if we give ice cream a pass in favor of some coffee and cake at the bakery?"

A bit embarrassed that she'd just made out like a hormonal teenager on Main Street, Angel stepped back and gestured to their clothing. "We're dripping wet."

He glanced down the street toward the bakery. "We can sit at the outside table since it's under a roof."

Considering they'd just get wetter if they headed back to their vehicles still parked at Gia's, she nodded. A hot coffee sounded good about right now.

When they reached the bakery, the blast of air-conditioning made her shiver. She reached up to rub her arms, but then Hunter put his arm around her shoulders and pulled her close to his side. He might be every bit as wet as she was, but just being held by him infused her with a warmth that was no doubt showing on her cheeks despite her complexion. Thank goodness Keri Teague, the owner of the bakery, wasn't working tonight. Instead, it was one of the high school students Keri had hired to work evenings so she and her sister-in-law Josephina could have more time with their families.

"What looks good?" Hunter asked.

You. But she didn't say that. Though he had to know based on how she'd darn near crawled up his body out on the sidewalk. Honestly, that was not like her at all. So much for easing back into dating, huh?

"Everything, but I think I'll take a slice of that strawberry cheesecake."

The pretty blonde behind the counter opened the sliding door on the back of the glass display case and pulled out the cheesecake while Hunter perused his choices, still not letting go of Angel. When the girl turned back for his order, he chose a slice of carrot cake.

"What, no chocolate?" Angel asked, thinking about how quickly he'd devoured his portion of her mom's chocolate cake and had continued to rave about it ever since.

He shrugged. "Feels like a night to be adventurous."

Part of her liked the sound of that, but another part wasn't quite ready to get any more adventurous than the rain-soaked PDA she'd already engaged in where anyone driving by could see.

Though she hated to lose the warmth and delicious weight of his arm around her shoulder, he removed it to pay for their desserts and coffees. When they stepped outside and sat at one of the two little tables on the sidewalk, the rain was still coming down in torrents. But under the protection of the roof, with a hot cup of coffee in hand and a handsome man across from her, Angel thought it felt more than a little like heaven.

Although she had to admit she was having trouble looking Hunter in the eye.

"You okay?"

"Yeah, why?"

"Because you're not actually eating your cheesecake, just cutting it into tiny pieces."

Maybe because her mind was decidedly elsewhere. She took a bite and savored the sweetness before swallowing.

"I'm a bit embarrassed," she said.

"Because we made out on Main Street?"

She glanced up to find him trying to hold a smile in check but failing miserably. "Yes. Is this one of those times when the guy feels half a foot taller because of his prowess?"

"Prowess, huh?" He did smile then, full and wide, tempting her to crawl across the table and have him for dessert instead.

Maybe she should go stand in the street until the rain cooled off her thoughts.

"If it makes you feel any better, I've never done anything like that, either." He paused. "But it felt right in the moment."

She forced herself to maintain eye contact and tell the truth, no matter how much her insides were somersaulting. "Yes, it did."

It still hadn't stopped raining by the time they finished their cakes.

"You stay here. I'll run up and get my truck, and come get you," Hunter said.

"You don't have to do that. It's not like I've dried out or anything."

"I'm trying to be chivalrous."

"Oh, in that case, please proceed." She smiled and made a sweeping hand gesture in the direction of Gia's.

He stood and walked to the edge of the building and the end of the roof. After a quick glance back at her, he took off running and disappeared around the corner. She couldn't help a girlish giggle, which she covered with her hand even though no one was nearby to hear her. While she waited for his return, she threw their trash away, then watched as the rain poured off the roof in a clear sheet. Hunter wasn't going to have a dry inch on his body anywhere. Without his or anyone else's eyes watching her, she allowed herself to imagine peeling off those clothes and toweling all that lean muscle dry.

She fanned her face at the mental image.

As she'd known he would be, when Hunter pulled up next to the curb and she hopped inside his truck he looked as if he'd taken a swim in the lake fully clothed.

"I'm sorry you're soaked again," she said.

"Last time I checked you don't control the weather." He pulled back out onto Main, his windshield wipers on full blast. "I would have been happy to sit with you at that little table and watch the rain all night, but I need to get home so Mildred, Sarah and Nina can head home themselves."

Guilt flooded Angel that over the course of the night, she'd managed to think very little about his mom.

"I shouldn't have kept you out so long. We could have just had the pizza and called it a night."

"No, everything's fine. I had a great time." He pulled into the lot at Gia's next to her truck. "I didn't realize how much I needed it."

She knew what he meant. She hadn't been able to let go of worries and responsibilities to the extent she had tonight since she'd found out she was pregnant with Julia.

"That makes two of us."

He put his truck in Park and looked toward her. "Did you enjoy it enough to do it again?"

"Yes."

"I don't know when I can get away again." From a lot of guys it would have sounded like an excuse, but she knew from Hunter it was the truth that came from a place of concern and responsibility some guys didn't even possess.

"That's okay. Life's a little more complicated than when we were teenagers."

"Ain't that the truth."

"In the meantime, let me know when's a good time to bring Julia over."

"How about tomorrow?"

Angel smiled. "No playing hard to get, huh?"

Hunter unfastened his seat belt and scooted closer to her. "Considering how long I've liked you, I don't want to waste any more time."

Was he thinking long-term commitment? That possibility, especially after only one date, caused her self-protective instincts to kick in. Maybe they were moving too fast. Or was she just paranoid because of her past failed relationships?

All her internal self-interrogation froze when he reached out and gently caressed her cheek.

"Can I kiss you good-night?"

His asking for permission touched her, especially after their hot and heavy kiss on the sidewalk. Did he sense her anxiety about moving too fast?

"I'd like that."

He pulled her close, running his fingers through her hair to the back of her head. When his lips touched hers, she told herself it would be a single sweet kiss to end

the night. But then that fire she'd felt earlier burst back
to full flame and she opened her mouth to him as her
hands gripped the front of his shirt.

Mercy, he tasted so good. Felt even better. Her entire
body felt as if it had just been awakened from hiberna-
tion by a shot of adrenaline straight to her sex drive.

She had no idea how long they kissed before she
somehow managed to pull away. Though she didn't want
to leave, if she didn't soon she was afraid she'd completely lose all grasp on common sense and start shuck-
ing clothes in Gia's parking lot. By the way Hunter was
breathing and how he looked at her, she suspected his
body was tempting him to do something similar.

"I think I better go," she said.

He nodded. "See you tomorrow?"

Should she see him again so soon, and with her
daughter in tow? "Yeah. I'll let you know what time."

Then before she could give in to Hunter Millbrook's
gravitational pull again, she retrieved her keys and made
a mad dash through the rain.

It was a slow drive back to the ranch, but she was
okay with that. She needed the time to calm down and
pull herself together so she didn't show up looking like
the hot, vibrating mass of unfulfilled need she was at
the moment. Though she normally didn't mind still living with her parents, tonight was one of those times she
wished she had her own place so she didn't have to face
anyone's curious gazes or outright questions.

Her lips still tingled with the aftereffects of their
kisses when she parked next to her dad's truck half an
hour later. She wondered if her parents would take one
look at her and be able to tell what she'd been doing.

She might be an adult with a child of her own, but

they were still her parents. She didn't want to know about their sex life, and certainly didn't want them to ponder hers. Were it not for how Julia adored living with her grandparents and how much they had loved and cared for Julia since her birth, Angel would give serious thought to getting her own place. But she couldn't rip them all apart just so she could save herself some embarrassment. Especially since there was no guarantee anything more than a few dates with Hunter would result from tonight's inaugural outing. Or even if she wanted it to.

Through the rain, she saw someone peek out the window. The height indicated it was none other than Julia, who was up past her bedtime. Even though the rain was coming down at a good clip, she retrieved the umbrella from the console—an umbrella that had done her no good earlier—and ran toward the house. On the porch, she shook off the umbrella before leaving it outside to dry. With a deep breath, she stepped inside to find Julia had retreated to the safety of her grandfather's lap.

"You know you still have a bedtime even though it's summer," Angel said to her daughter.

"But it's a special occasion. I wanted to ask you if you liked your date."

"It was fine. Now, off to bed or you'll be hating life in the morning."

Julia made the universal sound of frustration made by every child who wasn't ready to go to bed but had bumped up against the parent-prescribed bedtime.

"Go brush your teeth and put on your pajamas," Angel's mom said. "Then I'll come let you read to me."

Since Julia had learned to read, she didn't want bedtime stories read to her anymore. Instead, she liked to showcase her reading skills by being the reader.

As Julia reached her, Angel placed her hands atop her daughter's shoulders and kissed her on the top of her head. "I'll tell you about it in the morning, okay?"

Julia still wore her frustration, but she nodded. The moment she disappeared down the hall, Angel's mom shifted her expectant gaze to Angel.

"So, your date went well?" She looked so hopeful, as if the fate of all Angel's future happiness depended on her answer.

"We had a nice time—pizza at Gia's, then cake at the bakery." And yes, she was skipping the hot-and-heavy-kissing parts.

"Are you going out again?"

"Maybe. We'll see." The truth was there was a large part of her that would like to see him again right now, but she knew how her mom got her hopes up when one of her children started dating someone. Angel felt the weight of being the last one not happily married. She didn't want that kind of pressure, wanted instead to be able to take her time, to just have fun for a while without expectations from those around her. How realistic was it to jump from zero dating life to happily-ever-after in the span of a single date anyway?

She expected at least half a dozen more questions, but her mother surprised her by nodding and saying simply she was glad Angel had a good time before heading down the hall herself. Was she again treating Angel differently because of the whole situation with Dave?

"Well, that was surprisingly brief," Angel said once her mom was out of earshot.

"Don't let that fool you," her dad said with a chuckle as he lowered that week's issue of the *Blue Falls Gazette*.

Angel sighed before heading to the kitchen for a glass

of water. She was still standing by the sink when her dad came into the room.

"If you don't want your mother getting ahead of herself and beginning to plan a wedding, you might want to be, um, a little more careful."

At what must be a look of confusion on her face, he slid his phone across the countertop to her. She read a quick text from his buddy Abe Collins that revealed her hot kiss with Hunter on Main Street had been witnessed despite the driving rain. Reading that message with her dad standing right there caused embarrassment to flood every cell in her body.

"I'm sorry," she said.

"What for? You're a grown woman who's entitled to having a good time without others poking their noses into what isn't their business. And I told Abe exactly that."

Angel stared at her dad for a long moment before speaking. "Thank you."

"No need to thank me. I'm your dad. I want you to be happy. I don't care if you kiss someone in the middle of the Primrose Café during the lunch rush. Just know your mom might start hearing wedding bells if you do."

Angel gave her dad a big hug before heading for her room. Despite trying to not let any thoughts about weddings enter her mind, she couldn't keep them at bay entirely. In the safety of her room, she lay on the bed listening to the rain against her window. She allowed herself to imagine what life might be like with Hunter. He was kind, funny, a hard worker and one hell of a kisser. If he kissed like that, what else might he do really well?

Just the idea of a lifetime of slipping into bed with Hunter each night kept her awake a long time. And grateful Julia was in her own room instead of in the one where her mother was having thoughts so hot she wouldn't be surprised if she woke up to scorch marks on the sheets.

Chapter 8

The moment Hunter woke up and heard rain still hammering against the roof, he knew Angel's planned trip to his ranch to take photos was a no-go. That soured his mood more than knowing he had to get out and work in the miserable weather, so much so that he lay in bed a good half hour longer than he normally did. But then the sounds of his mom moving about the house penetrated his mental replay of his date with Angel and he leaped from the bed. He threw on a pair of shorts and a T-shirt before heading to the kitchen, where he expected to find her. When he didn't, he hurried through the rest of the house. Still not finding her, he felt his heart begin hammering against his ribs. Had she gotten confused and wandered outside into the rain?

He jerked open the front door, ready to call out to her before noticing her sitting in one of the rocking chairs, cup of coffee in hand. He thought he might pass out in relief when she smiled at him, her eyes bright.

"I can't remember the last time you slept in," she said. "Must have been some date last night."

He quickly hid his fear for her, not wanting to bring up her disease when she seemed happy and clearheaded this morning. Instead, he sank into the other rocker and gestured at the rain still falling. "Took me longer to get home last night."

And when he'd arrived, his mom was tired and had only asked him if he'd had a good time. He'd been relieved when Mildred told him they'd had fun and his mom had been fine and perfectly lucid the entire evening.

"Yes, I'm sure the rainy drive home was what's been on your mind this morning."

Okay, he wasn't having this conversation with his mom. Just the idea of her identifying the thoughts that had been running through his head this morning made him distinctly uncomfortable.

"I better get dressed. The animals aren't going to feed themselves."

She motioned for him to keep his seat. "Don't worry about that. I've already fed the horses and the chickens and gathered the eggs. I didn't muck the stalls, but that can wait a little longer while you indulge your mom in tales of your evening."

"We had a nice time." More than nice. He hadn't stopped thinking about how Angel had felt in his arms, how she'd tasted on his lips, since. Not even while he'd been sleeping, evidently, judging by the bits of dreams he remembered and the state in which he'd awakened.

"I think you are deliberately understating things."

"What makes you say that?"

"You've liked her for a long time and when you left to meet her, I don't think I've ever seen you so nervous."

He didn't want to lie to his mom about how much he liked Angel, but he didn't want to get her hopes up, either.

"If that girl has a lick of sense, you don't have anything to worry about," she said.

"It was just a first date, Mom." Sure, it had gone really well, but that didn't mean Angel felt the same way he did or that she wouldn't be embarrassed by her actions in the light of day.

"Your dad and I started out as just a first date."

"Yes, but you were friends before that. Angel and I had barely ever spoken to each other."

"Say what you will, I have faith."

He knew once his mom set her mind on something, there was little chance of changing it so he didn't try. Besides, he hoped she was right. Instead, he stood, dropped a kiss atop her head, then went to get dressed for another day of work keeping their ranch afloat.

As soon as he stepped into his bedroom, his phone dinged with a text. He suspected he knew what it said before he picked it up and saw the message was from Angel.

Rain check on the trip out to your ranch?

He had to smile at her phrasing and the smiley face that accompanied the text despite the disappointment he'd known was coming.

Sure, he texted back. Standing invitation.

Even though he couldn't reasonably expect Angel to

come out to take photos in such soggy weather, he nevertheless found himself in a mood that matched the dark gray sky as he first mucked out the stalls, then changed the oil in his truck. Halfway through the morning, he headed to the house to get a drink and casually check on his mom. He found her in the kitchen in the middle of making a big pot of chili, the perfect rainy-weather food.

"Oh, good, I was about to come find you. Just got a call that your tractor part came in, and as luck would have it I need some chili powder. I evidently forgot to put it on the list after I used the last of the previous bottle."

At least changing the fuel pump on the tractor was something else he could do in the dry confines of the barn.

"Okay," he said. "I won't be gone long."

"I'll be fine." She held up her index finger. "I just remembered I have a couple of books on hold at the library, too."

By the time he made all the required stops in town, his stomach was growling. A big bowl of chili was going to hit the spot. As he headed back down Main Street, he couldn't help smiling when he drove past where he'd kissed Angel the night before. He'd never be able to pass the furniture store again without remembering the feel of her warm mouth beneath his. As if thinking about her had made her appear, he noticed her sitting outside the bakery at the same table where they'd eaten cake the night before.

Well, his day just got a hundred times better. And luck was on his side since he was able to whip into an available parking space across the street. But as he reached to turn off the engine, he saw someone approach the table. Though the rain had lessened, it still took him a few seconds of looking through the drizzle to figure out who it was.

His breath caught when he realized it was Chris Ross. Maybe he was just saying hello while Angel waited for someone else—her mom, Sloane, a friend—who was inside the bakery. But in the next moment, Angel gestured to the other seat and her ex-boyfriend sat in the same chair Hunter had occupied less than twenty-four hours before.

He was aware he didn't know the whole story, that he wasn't even entitled to it after only one date, but that didn't keep him from wondering. And feeling that once again fate was throwing up a roadblock between him and a relationship with Angel. Or at least the possibility of one.

With a sigh, he put the truck in gear and pulled back out onto the street. He tried to think about anything but why Angel and Chris might be meeting, what they could be talking about, but it proved useless. Despite his determination to not jump to conclusions, part of his mind refused to stop whispering that his chance with Angel was slipping away. That when he eventually lost his mother, there would be no one beside him to help bear the pain. And he would be completely alone.

Angel attempted not to fidget as she sat facing Chris, tried and failed not to think about how only last night she'd sat at this same table across from Hunter, the happiest she'd been in a long time.

"Thanks for meeting me," Chris said. "I wasn't sure you would."

"To be honest, neither was I. But my curiosity won the day."

"I'm glad it did." He glanced through the window where the bakery was doing a brisk business. Keri had told her once that rainy days made people want sweets and coffee, no matter the time of year. "What would you like?"

"I'm good."

"You sure?"

She nodded. "But you go ahead."

While her curiosity was carving a tunnel through her brain, what would a few more minutes matter? The rain had already ruined her plans for the day anyway.

Chris stood. "Be right back."

He seemed off somehow, maybe jittery, which made no sense and didn't seem like the Chris she'd once known.

While he was inside, Angel sat back and watched the traffic roll by. Her thoughts wandered to Hunter again, as they repeatedly had since the moment she'd driven away from him the night before. Their date had been great, but if she was being honest it had scared her a bit, too. Scared her how quickly her attraction to Hunter was building, how thrilling his kisses had been, how she feared falling for him too fast and too hard, just as she had with Dave. No matter how many times she told herself that Hunter wasn't like Dave, a little voice of doubt in her head whispered, "You don't know that for sure."

But one thing she was sure of was that she loved how it felt being with Hunter last night. Laughing during their failed attempt to outrun the rain. Kissing with abandon as if no one could possibly see them. And the way he'd stood up to Danny even though he'd acknowledged he knew she was perfectly capable of fighting her own battles was just…sexy. Odd to think of facing off against a bigot as sexy, but it was. It showed what kind of man he was, what sort of heart beat within his finely toned chest.

Chris's sinking onto the chair opposite her again startled her out of her daydream about unbuttoning Hunter's shirt to see what she'd felt the night before. Once again she was thankful for her complexion because otherwise everyone on Main Street would see the heat in her cheeks.

She looked at the coffee and oatmeal-cranberry cookie Chris had placed in front of her.

"I remembered you liked those," he said, pointing to the cookie.

"How could you possibly remember that?"

"I remember lots of things." He paused and lowered his gaze for a moment before lifting it back to hers. "Like how badly I treated you. That's why I wanted to talk to you, to apologize."

Angel just stared, not knowing quite what to think. He was apologizing an entire decade after he'd cheated on her?

"Angel?"

"Uh, I'm surprised." She considered him for a moment, how he'd been away from Blue Falls for years only to come back now. And he was apologizing for old wrongs. She leaned forward. "Are you an alcoholic?"

Confusion flooded Chris's face. "Huh?"

"Your apology, is it part of one of those twelve-step programs?"

"Oh. No, not really, though I guess it might be one of my own making." He glanced toward the street, but his expression said he was looking far beyond the cars and pedestrians. "I've just been doing a lot of thinking lately, wanting to make up for the things I've done wrong in my life." He shifted his attention back to her. "And one of the worst things I did was cheat on you. I wish I could take it back. You didn't deserve to be treated like that."

Angel remembered how badly his betrayal had hurt, how she'd cried until her head felt as if it would crack open along with her heart. But she'd moved on, and it felt juvenile and petty to resurrect an old grudge now.

"It was a long time ago. Kids do stupid things."

"Be that as it may, I'm still sorry."

She smiled, and she found the smile was surprisingly genuine. The layer of teenage cockiness Chris had once worn was no longer in evidence, as if it had never existed or been deliberately scrubbed away.

"Apology accepted."

Chris exhaled, his relief obvious.

"Did you think I was still angry after all this time?"

"You wouldn't be the first person to hold a grudge that long, myself included."

"Who were you ticked at?"

He didn't answer at first, instead taking a drink of his coffee. As he sat the cup back slowly onto the table, he said, "Let's just say that my parents and I were not on the best of terms when I left for college."

"Really? I had no idea."

"Mom and Dad are very good at keeping up appearances."

Okay, even if his parents were on his apology tour, there was still bitterness on Chris's end. Her curiosity ate at her some more, but she kept quiet. They were not close friends, and that seemed like a close-friends kind of question to ask.

He seemed to climb out of whatever negative well he'd fallen into and smiled. Only then did she realize that even though Chris had grown up to be a handsome man, he also looked tired, as if he hadn't gotten enough sleep in a long time.

"Are you okay?"

His smile wavered. "Sure. This is nice."

Angel leaned her forearms on the table, her curiosity telling her better sense to take a long hike.

"Why apologize after all this time?"

Chris stared into his coffee as if the liquid might reveal the answer to her question.

"I lost someone recently, and it made me realize how short life can be."

"I'm sorry."

She spotted a momentary glimpse of a smile before it was gone. "Thanks." He sighed and gripped his cup. "I started thinking that I haven't always been the best person and I needed to change that."

"I can understand coming home to see people, but why move back? I heard through the grapevine that you liked Oregon."

"I did. I still do. It's just…full of raw memories right now. And, well, even though I suspect it'll be the second hardest thing I've ever done, I need to try to repair my relationship with my parents."

She suspected the hardest thing was saying goodbye to the person he'd loved and lost. "Were you married?"

He gave a slight shake of his head. "We talked about it, but time wasn't on our side."

She thought about Hunter losing his father when he was barely out of high school, how he was going to lose his mom before he actually lost her. Time could be cruel.

"How about you? Are you seeing anyone?"

He couldn't possibly want to go out with her again, could he? Was that why he was apologizing to her, in the hope that the apology would pave the way to his asking her out for more than coffee?

No, the sorrow she'd seen on his face and heard in his voice weren't feigned.

"I'm not sure."

Chris tilted his head and gave her an amused look.

"I'm not officially dating anyone," she said, "but I did go on a date last night."

Chris smiled. "And it went well?"

No matter how crazy it was to be sitting here talking to an ex-boyfriend about someone she wouldn't mind being a current boyfriend, she found herself doing exactly that.

"Better than expected."

"Anyone I know?"

"Hunter Millbrook. He was ahead of us in school."

"I saw him at the hardware store the other day. Good guy?"

"Yeah." She didn't hesitate and that told her a lot about what she knew deep down.

"I'm happy for you." Though Chris smiled again, he couldn't totally hide how he wished he could have romantic happiness himself.

"What was her name?"

"Who?"

"The woman you lost."

Chris sat back in his chair, and Angel thought he might actually get up and leave. Had she crossed a line? Or was the loss so fresh he couldn't talk about it?

"Darren."

Angel's first thought was that she liked that name for a girl, but then she registered the apprehension on Chris's face, as if he thought she might stalk off at the realization that Darren was, in fact, a guy. And then everything fell into place—why she and he hadn't worked out, why he'd moved so far away from Blue Falls and...

"That's why you've been estranged from your parents?"

He nodded and she'd swear she heard him sigh in relief.

"I'm sorry."

He shrugged. "Part of me thinks I'm crazy for coming back here, especially now. People don't tend to change."

"Sometimes they do." She gestured toward him, indicating he was doing the very thing he claimed people rarely did.

Chris took a big gulp of coffee as if it were a good, stiff drink known for giving courage. She hated that not everyone was fortunate to have the kind of understanding parents she did.

"Maybe they'll surprise me." The way he said it indicated he didn't hold out much hope, which made her admire him for trying despite believing he'd likely fail.

She suspected that in the wake of his loss, he needed his family as anyone would in the same situation. When Dave had left, leaving her alone to face pregnancy and then single motherhood, her family had gotten her through the scary, heartbroken days that followed. They hadn't made her feel shame, but she deduced Chris could not say the same.

If his relationship with his family was going to be such a trial, the guy needed friends. She wondered how many of his friends from high school who were still around knew about his orientation. And, if they did, would they be any more supportive than his parents?

"Do you mind me asking what happened?" She

thought he meant he'd lost Darren to death, but she wasn't sure. It could have just been a horrible breakup, but her gut told her otherwise.

"Wrong place, wrong time. He was on his way to work and got hit…" His voice hitched and he paused to swallow visibly. "He was hit by a tractor trailer."

A horrible image formed in Angel's mind, and she wished she could wind back time for Chris and Darren. It wasn't the first time she'd had that wish, but that wasn't the way life worked. She and all of her siblings had lived through their own losses or abuses, but it had made them the people they were. Still, she didn't want to think about any of them losing their spouses. The pain would be unbearable.

Her thoughts shifted to Hunter. They weren't married, had only gone on one date, but the thought of something happening to him made her chest ache.

"I know this won't help, but I'm really sorry."

"Thanks." He took a deep breath, as if trying to shove off some of the weight of his grief.

A few long moments of silence passed as Chris seemed to sink into his thoughts and Angel tried to think of the best thing to say. She decided to take a chance that Chris might like to talk about Darren, especially if his parents weren't supportive and he couldn't talk about him with them.

"How did you two meet?"

She breathed easier when Chris smiled. "A stray cat brought us together."

"This sounds like an interesting story."

Chris fiddled with his cup. "I worked in marketing for a big retailer, and when I left work one day I found this skinny little kitten huddled under my car to get out of the rain. It took some coaxing, but I got her to come to me. She was skin and bones, but had the bluest eyes you've ever seen. I went straight to the vet my neighbor used, and the moment I saw him I just knew."

"The vet was Darren."

He nodded. "There was an instant connection, although Darren didn't acknowledge it for a while. He'd just gone through a bad breakup and wasn't keen on dating again anytime soon."

"But you convinced him otherwise?"

"It took a couple of months, but I can be persistent when I want something...or someone." He smiled. "Persistent in a non-restraining-order sort of way."

"Always the best way."

"How about you? I don't remember you and Hunter being friends before."

"We weren't. When I was at the gallery preparing for my exhibit he was working on the roof. And he may have almost knocked me in the head with a two-by-four."

"That's certainly a drastic way to get someone's attention."

She ended up telling him pretty much the entire story of her and Hunter so far and was surprised by how easy it was to talk to him about things she hadn't told anyone else. She never would have predicted this scenario.

As they talked, she noticed the occasional glance their way, a few conversations between passersby that no doubt were filled with speculation about the two of them. She wondered if he'd noticed as well because he stood and gathered up their trash. With work of her own to get back to, she also stood.

After Chris returned from tossing their trash into

the outdoor can, a bit of awkwardness sprang up between them.

"It was good to see you," she said, hoping to dispel it.

"You, too. Thanks for meeting me." The look on his face was less tense than when he'd arrived.

"Anytime," she said, and she meant it. Continuing to go with her instincts, she gave him a quick hug. "Seriously, if you need to talk more or just want to hang out, let me know."

"I may take you up on that."

As Angel walked back to her truck, she realized that she felt lighter, as if some little part of her heart that had been in shadow was now benefiting from direct sunlight despite the rain that was still falling. She smiled as she slid into the driver's seat. Life was looking pretty good right now, and damn if she wasn't going to enjoy every single minute of it. As soon as the rain gave way to sun again, she was going out to Hunter's ranch in search of one of those fantastic kisses she hadn't known she needed in her life.

Chapter 9

Once upon a time, Texas had a drought. But it wasn't over the past week. And Hunter's mood matched the soggy, muddy world he went to work in every day. He'd texted a couple of times with Angel, but she'd said nothing further about coming to the ranch. Not that Mother Nature was cooperating anyway. Add in the fact that he kept imagining her with Chris, and yeah, even the cattle didn't want to be near him.

"Have you asked out Angel again?" his mom asked the moment his bottom hit the chair at the kitchen table.

He sighed as she placed a plate of scrambled eggs and sausage in front of him. Either she was being annoyingly persistent or she'd forgotten she'd asked him the same question the night before. He didn't want to answer, no matter which was true.

"Well?" she prompted when he didn't respond.

"We've both been busy."

She huffed in frustration, but to his surprise she turned around and left the room. He took the opportunity to shovel down his breakfast and hurry out the back door before she could launch into round two.

Though the rain had finally lessened to no more than a mist, the day still felt heavy with grayness. He put on his hat and headed toward the barn. He was nearly at the entrance when he heard the sound of a vehicle coming up the drive. When he glanced in that direction, it took him a few moments to realize that the truck that emerged from the thin layer of fog belonged to none other than Angel Hartley.

There was no sun in sight, but his mood lifted as if it was high noon on a bright first day of summer. Then he remembered how she'd looked sitting across from Chris, and the bottom fell out of his good mood.

But he'd said she could come out and take photos, that Julia could visit with his mom, and he was a man of his word. When she waved, he waved back and wasn't able to prevent his heart rate from accelerating as he watched her park and then hop out of the truck with a smile on her face.

He walked toward her as she came around to the passenger side to help Julia out.

"I hope you don't mind us showing up without me calling first," Angel said as he drew close. "We needed to get out of the house. Been going a bit stir-crazy this week with all the rain."

"It's fine, though I doubt you'll get many good pictures."

"Oh, I don't know. This type of weather can convey a different mood."

"Yeah, soggy."

She smiled. "If I'm to show the truth of the ranching life in my photos, they can't all be full of sunshine. The work doesn't stop just because the weather isn't optimal."

The front door to the house opened and his mom hurried out to greet their guests with a wave and a big smile that helped alleviate some of his sour mood. Seeing Julia reciprocate with an enthusiastic wave and smile of her own helped a bit more.

A snippet that he'd heard on some show his mom had been watching the day before landed in the front of his mind. Something about every day being what you make it, so why not make it great. As a rule he wasn't into all that self-reflective, self-help stuff, but he supposed a positive attitude never hurt anybody. And he had to admit he really liked seeing Angel again.

His mom whopped him on the arm when she reached them. "Why didn't you tell me we were going to have company?" She paused. "Or—"

"I didn't tell you because I didn't know." He'd heard the question before she spoke it, her wondering if maybe he had and it had made a hasty departure from her mind like things often did.

"I hope we're not intruding," Angel said.

"Nonsense," his mom replied. "I had a mind to make some cookies today, so now I have even more of a reason."

"Cookies!" Julia clapped in excitement.

Angel rested her hand atop her daughter's head in obvious affection. "I think you have a fan."

His mom held out her hand for Julia to take. "Let's get out of this dismal weather, then."

In the next moment, the two strode off toward the

house as if they'd known each other forever. A wave of affection for Julia filled his heart.

"You have a great kid there," he said to Angel once the others were out of earshot.

"Yeah, I got really lucky in that department."

He looked over at Angel, and it hit him anew how beautiful she was. "It's more than luck. You're a good role model."

She shifted her gaze to his. "Thank you. That means a lot."

"So, how does this work?"

"Huh?"

The way she was looking up at him made him want to pull her close and kiss her like she'd never been kissed, so that it would make her forget all about Chris or any other man. But after seeing her with Chris, he had no idea where he stood. Maybe he was making something big out of nothing.

When he realized he hadn't answered her, he broke eye contact and nodded in the general direction of the barn. "I have to go feed the horses, but I doubt that's photo-worthy."

"Depends. Some people are photogenic no matter what they're doing."

Okay, was he that terrible at reading women, or was she flirting with him?

"If you can make feeding and mucking stalls look like art, then you're even more talented than I thought." Before he could act on his desire to pull her close, he turned and headed toward the barn.

Angel didn't immediately follow Hunter. Something was off with him. Was he annoyed that she'd shown up unannounced? Or was it something about his mom, though she'd seemed perfectly fine when she'd come outside to greet her and Julia? Maybe despite his invitation, he hadn't thought she'd take him up on it. Could she have read him wrong the night of their date? It certainly wouldn't be the first time she'd thought a man felt affection for her only to discover she'd overestimated how much.

Well, she couldn't very well turn around and leave when they'd just arrived and Julia was in full-on I'm-going-to-have-cookies mode. So she grabbed her camera bag from the front seat of the truck and hurried to catch up to the man she'd been fantasizing about almost nonstop since their date.

"Did you hear about the flooding out at the Granger place?" she asked as she entered the barn and found she didn't know what else to say to Hunter.

Over the next several minutes, she brought up a wide range of topics to which Hunter responded with minimal replies. His mind seemed to be on the other side of the world, quite possibly on a different planet. He was like a different person from who he'd been the last time she'd seen him. All the fantasies of her arriving here today and having Hunter kiss her until her knees buckled evaporated, leaving a hollow place in her chest that she'd thought she might finally be able to fill.

A tinge of anger caused her to clench her jaw as she adjusted the settings on the camera. Before their date, she hadn't fully realized that empty space had been there in the first place. But now that she was aware of it, it demanded to be filled. Damn Hunter for shining a big, bright spotlight on something that had been just fine hiding away in a dark corner.

Though part of her wanted to lash out at him, she reined in her impulse and took a step down a less confrontational path.

"Is everything okay with your mom?"

He looked up from where he was filling a stall with fresh straw. "As much as it can be. Why? Are you afraid for Julia to be alone with her?"

She actually hadn't thought about that. Should she have? "No, but you seem to be preoccupied. If this isn't a good idea, let me know and I'll go to the house and get Julia. I don't want us being here to be an imposition."

"I told you it was fine."

"And yet you're acting as if you'd rather be on the face of the moon." She couldn't quite contain her irritation, despite her best efforts. "I thought we had a good time the other night, but if I was wrong, just tell me."

He turned to face her fully, his hand wrapped around the handle of the upright pitchfork and a look of confusion on his face. "So you'd still like to go out with me again?"

Now she was the one confused. "Yes. Why wouldn't I?"

"I thought maybe it was a onetime thing, that you might be going out with someone else, too."

"Seriously? You're the first person I've gone out with in ages. I—" She stopped when the fact that she lived in a small town where the grapevine was extensive and well used hit her. "Someone told you about me having coffee with Chris, didn't they?"

Hunter stepped out of the stall and crossed the center aisle to hang the pitchfork on the opposite wall. "Actually, I saw you."

"Oh."

"Listen, it's no big deal. It's not like we're a couple. You can date whoever you want."

Was he actually jealous? She knew she should be irritated that he might feel possessive after only a single date, but her instincts told her he wasn't—at least not in the scary way. But if he liked her enough to be jealous of another man… She didn't know if it made her weak or pitiful, but she liked the feeling. It'd been so long since someone had liked her enough to be jealous. Actually, she wasn't sure anyone ever had been.

"You know, you're right. I can go out with whomever I like." The flicker of a defeated look that passed over Hunter's face before he hid it and moved to close the stall door showed her he was indeed jealous. "That's why I chose to go out with you and would like to again—unless, of course, you've got someone else *you'd* rather be with." She couldn't resist teasing him a little.

"No," Hunter said quickly as he turned back toward her just as she closed the distance between them.

Hunter's breath seemed to catch, and she had to admit hers did, as well. In the next moment, Hunter's hands gripped her shoulders. She saw the question in his eyes, and he must have seen the answer in hers because he lowered his lips to hers and gave her the sweetest kiss of her life. But that sweetness was deceptive because it lit a fuse and she inhaled sharply as the kiss deepened into a twin of the one they'd shared beside Main Street as the heavens had opened up. A surge of desire flooded her and she opened more widely to him.

Hunter moaned in response, causing her to press closer against him. He stumbled, his back hitting the stall and causing the horse to snort and shy away in response.

Hunter laughed against her needy mouth. "I thought it was the guy who was supposed to sweep the girl off her feet."

"It's the twenty-first century. Times change." After all, she'd been the one to ask him out first. And at the moment, she was very glad she had.

Even though she knew there was the possibility that Hunter's mom or Julia could walk into the barn at any moment, she couldn't tear herself away from him. And he seemed equally unwilling to stop, much to her body's delight. Heaven help her, if they were alone on this ranch she might be tempted to find out if the barn had an empty stall and a fresh pile of hay. Sure, hay was itchy, but she suspected being with Hunter would be worth some poking and itching.

As it was, she was afraid she might burst into flames and burn the barn down. That sure wasn't a great way to take a relationship to the next level.

The thought of a relationship jolted her so much that she broke the kiss and took a step back without thinking.

"You okay?" The concern in Hunter's voice and visible in his expression nearly made her walk right back into his arms, but she managed to refrain.

They'd been out only once, and already she was thinking about a relationship? But was that bad? She really felt that he was a great guy, the kind you dreamed about but couldn't quite believe existed. She'd had relationships before, but they'd never ended well. She'd dreamed of happily-ever-after, but Dave had shot a giant, gaping hole in her belief in that. At least for her.

But maybe her view on that was changing. Not only did she have her parents as a prime example of lifelong love, but all four of her siblings were now happily married.

And damn if she didn't want that for herself. She just had to be sure this time. One hundred percent certain. Julia deserved that. Angel deserved that.

"I'm fine," she finally said. "Just got a bit carried away."

Hunter's concern slowly faded into a smile. "That makes two of us."

"We keep doing that and we're going to get caught."

He took a step toward her and caressed her cheek. "I wouldn't mind as long as that meant I got to keep kissing you."

"You do know the right things to say to a girl."

"Really? Good to know since I haven't had a lot of practice."

She shook her head. "How is that possible? You're quite the catch."

His eyes widened, as if she'd truly shocked him.

"I don't know about that."

"I do." She lifted onto her toes and placed a gentle kiss on his still-wet lips. Man, she liked those lips. She suspected it might be a bit too easy to love them.

"Maybe catch and release," he said with a self-deprecating grin.

Angel barely kept herself from saying that she never wanted to release him. She wasn't ready to tell him anything that serious. She wasn't even ready to fully admit it to herself.

Instead, she smiled and playfully swatted him on the arm. "Now you're just being silly."

Worried the conversation might turn serious, she eased away from him and retrieved her camera from where she'd left it atop a hay bale.

"I came here to take photos." She motioned around the interior of the barn. "Do cowboy things, cowboy."

He chuckled and gave her a look that made her body heat. "Seems photos aren't the only thing you came here for."

Her mouth fell open like some exaggerated cartoon character. Despite his most excellent kissing skills, the teasing seemed out of character. But she couldn't deny she liked it. Maybe he was just more comfortable with her now, less guarded. It made her wonder what else he might say or do if they grew even closer.

Angel stared at the photo of Hunter on her computer screen, knowing she'd never offer it for sale. The smile he wore felt too personal, too intimate, even in profile. She'd captured the shot right after Julia had brought Angel and Hunter cookies fresh from Evelyn's oven, then hurried back to the house.

These are delicious, she'd said. *It's official. Surrounded by so many great bakers, I'm never going to be able to compete.*

You have other talents.

On the surface, Hunter could have meant her photography. But that smile had held a bit of naughtiness, and damn if her lady parts hadn't throbbed in response. Before she'd left to collect Julia and head home, they'd throbbed even more when she'd been the one with her back against the barn wall and Hunter's mouth threatening to consume her whole.

"I like Hunter."

Angel yelped at the sound of Julia's voice so close. "Goodness, you scared the daylights out of me."

Julia giggled as if that was the funniest thing she'd ever heard.

Angel pulled her daughter onto her lap, keenly aware

that the amount of time left during which she'd be able to do that without Julia protesting was dwindling.

"I thought you were reading."

"I'm done. I need more books."

Julia was quite the fan of the summer reading program at the library. In fact, she was on track to read more than any of the other kids and summer vacation had barely started.

"Okay, Miss Speedy, we'll go to the library tomorrow."

"Can't we go today?"

"No, sweetie. I need to work. I have to pick out some new photos to put in a gallery in Austin." Another opportunity that had come from her opening at Merline's gallery. She still hadn't heard back from her submission to *West*, but she was trying not to fret about it. No news was good news, right?

"Can I help?"

"Sure. I'll go through the photos and you tell me which ones you like."

Julia pointed toward the screen. "I like that one."

Angel did, too. A lot. But she said, "It doesn't quite work. The lighting isn't right."

In fact, there was absolutely nothing wrong with the lighting. It was a great photo, but it was hers. She didn't want to share it, irrationally afraid that doing so would cause her to lose him and whatever it was that was growing between them. She imagined women seeing that photo and falling instantly in love. Scary as it was, she thought she was likely headed that direction herself.

"He's handsome."

Angel was shocked to hear that phrase come out of her young daughter's mouth, but Julia wasn't wrong. "Yes, he is."

"Do you like him?"

"Yes, he's very nice."

"Is he your boyfriend now?"

Okay, this kid was full of surprises today. "No. Well, not really. We went out on a date, and we had fun. Would it bother you if he was my boyfriend?"

"Nope. You smile a lot when you're with him."

Angel's heart squeezed. "Do I not smile enough when I'm not around Hunter?"

Julia shrugged. "You smile and laugh, but you do it more with him." She grinned. "I think you *like* him."

Angel didn't know how to respond, didn't want to commit too much when it was still so early in her relationship with Hunter. But she also didn't want to lie to Julia.

"I do like him."

Julia giggled again and kissed Angel on the cheek before hopping off her lap and hurrying for the door. Kids' interest in conversations shifted so quickly. As she watched Julia head off to whatever had drawn her away, Angel spotted Sloane leaning against the edge of the doorway with an I-knew-it grin on her face.

No sense navigating off the picture on her computer or even closing it now because her sister had no doubt seen it and heard a significant part of her conversation with Julia.

"Hey, Aunt Sloane," Julia said as she hurried out the door.

Sloane ruffled Julia's straight, dark hair. "Hey, kiddo."

After Julia disappeared down the hall, Sloane ambled into the room and flopped down on Angel's bed, making herself right at home even though she didn't live there anymore.

Angel made a let's-have-it motion with her hand. "Go ahead."

"I'm sure I don't know what you're talking about," Sloane said with a smile so full of mischief it was almost its own sentient being.

"You are so full of it."

"But you love me."

"Some days."

Sloane rolled onto her side and propped her head against her upturned head. "You're falling for the guy, aren't you?"

"What makes you say that?"

Sloane pointed at the photo of Hunter on the computer screen. "That's not like your other photos. It feels personal."

Because it was.

Angel glanced at the photo. "Maybe. That's equal parts exciting and scary."

"Focus on the exciting and tell the scary to take a jump off the nearest cliff."

"Easier said than done."

"True, but it'll be worth it."

"How do you know that?"

"Because I'm incredibly smart."

Angel rolled her eyes at her sister.

"Seriously, after all the years since Dave hightailed it, you've been a great mom, a great daughter, an okay sister—"

Angel threw a rainbow-colored Koosh ball at her sister. Sloane laughed as she batted it away, but then her expression grew more serious.

"It's time you focus on yourself and what makes you

happy. And don't tell me photography makes you happy. I know that. But it's not holding you at night."

Sloane wasn't wrong.

"I wish I could turn off the part of my brain that makes me worry things will go horribly wrong."

"Unfortunately, it doesn't work that way. You just have to dive in and hope for the best. I don't think Hunter is going anywhere and he seems to like Julia, so he already has more going for him than Dave did." She ended by calling Dave a rather unflattering name, which made Angel snort out a laugh.

After Sloane left to do some prep work for her next ranch camp, Angel sat staring at the photo of Hunter. She let her fingertips drift over the image, pausing on his lips. The mere thought of him made her entire body buzz, and not just in a sexual way. It was as if a part of her had been asleep since Dave had left her and was only now awakening again. She didn't know if Dave had damaged that part of her or if she'd unconsciously turned a switch within herself for the purpose of self-preservation, but she didn't want any part of herself closed off anymore.

She liked how she felt when she was with Hunter, even when they were just talking and laughing. And he seemed to feel the same. It wasn't only the steamy kisses they'd shared, although she didn't think she'd ever get tired of those. Her heart accelerated as much whenever his hand grazed hers, or if he looked at her in a certain way—as if she was the most beautiful and mesmerizing creature on the planet. She'd never known she could feel that way or that anyone could ever look at her with that kind of expression.

As she stared at his profile, she saw no deception

there. She didn't believe he was the kind of person to say one thing to her while thinking another. She now suspected Chris had done it out of confusion or self-preservation, but Dave had lied by omission for truly selfish reasons. No matter their reasoning, they'd both abandoned her—the same as her birth mother. Despite their reasons, it still hurt and carved away a part of the person being abandoned.

True, she still didn't know everything there was to know about Hunter, but he seemed solid, steady, honest. And like Sloane had said, she didn't see him suddenly disappearing. Which was good news because Angel was pretty sure she was falling for him.

She just hoped he was there to catch her instead of letting her face plant on the ground as he walked away.

Chapter 10

Angel held Hunter's hand as they climbed the park trail that led to an overlook with a gorgeous view of Blue Falls Lake and the surrounding Hill Country. Over the past two weeks, they'd spent as much time together as possible, which usually meant that she went out to his ranch or she met him in town for a quick lunch or cup of coffee because he was understandably concerned about leaving his mom alone for too long. But today, Mildred had offered to take Evelyn first to a doctor's appointment, then to the hair salon and finally out to lunch. A girls' day that had the added benefit of giving Hunter a break, time to spend with Angel.

When they reached the overlook, she was breathing heavily. She could blame it on the climb, but she was in pretty good shape. Honestly, her need for more oxygen had more to do with the fact that she and Hunter were more alone than they'd ever been. And every time she was with him, she was more certain she was falling in love. Each time it became a bit easier to push her doubts and concerns away. He'd given her no reason to believe he was anything other than what he seemed on the surface—a good man who was crazy about her. She now understood the phrase "drunk on love" because sometimes she felt unsteady around him.

When they reached the top of the trail and the trees lining it gave way to the expansive view, she was struck anew by the beauty of her little slice of the world.

"I don't think I could ever get tired of this view," she said as she gradually caught her breath.

"Me, neither."

But when she glanced over at him, she realized he wasn't talking about the panorama in front of them. He was staring at her.

"You know you could have had that view without hiking up this trail," she said with a smile.

"Yeah, but I wanted you all to myself." He pulled her into his arms and dropped a tender kiss on her lips, one that gradually heated until his hands were threaded through her hair and she was gripping the front of his shirt as if she might topple off the cliff if she didn't hang on.

When they finally came up for air, she placed her cheek against his chest. "That never gets old."

"No, it doesn't." He settled a kiss atop her head.

They stood that way for a bit longer before the sound of voices coming up the trail intruded.

"So much for being alone, huh?" she said.

He made a sound of frustration, but took her hand and led her to the edge of the overlook as a family of four came into view.

"It really is beautiful up here," she said.

"Yeah, makes you realize how lucky we are."

Angel's heart expanded. He couldn't know how much it meant to her to hear him say that after the last man she'd been serious about had left Blue Falls, her and his child behind as if none of them meant anything to him.

"What is it?" Hunter asked.

She looked over at him, wondering if he could detect the truth in her eyes. Part of her wanted him to, but another part was scared to say the words yet. What if despite how he seemed to feel about her his feelings weren't as deep as hers? She didn't want to scare him off before those feelings might eventually deepen to the point hers already occupied.

"I'm just glad you almost hit me with that two-by-four at the gallery."

He smiled. "I wish it hadn't taken almost injuring you for you to get up the guts to ask me out."

"But I did. That's all that matters." She wanted to kiss him again. In truth, she wanted a lot more than that. But the top of a public trail with a vacationing family close by didn't seem the best place to take their relationship to the next level.

She considered how difficult it was for him to find time away from home, how he had no one else to help shoulder all the burdens he had to bear, and wondered if they'd ever be able to grab more than a couple of stolen hours here and there. She had to believe the universe hadn't brought them together only to keep them just enough apart to be endlessly frustrating.

As the family marveled over the view and took a series of selfies with the glimmering lake in the background, Hunter took her hand and led her to a nearby bench.

"I have something I want to give you," he said once they were seated.

"Oh?" Her mind raced, trying to figure out what it might be.

When he pulled a small envelope from his pocket and extended it to her, her mind skidded around a corner toward what could fit in an envelope. He didn't seem like the poem-writing type. A lottery ticket seemed... well, odd.

"What is it?"

"Open it and find out."

Was it her imagination or did he look nervous? Okay, that officially made her nervous, too, as she took the envelope and opened it. Inside was a woman's name and phone number.

"I don't understand." She looked up at Hunter to find him watching her.

"She was a nurse at the hospital when you were left there. She remembers you."

Angel felt as if a huge boulder made of ice settled in her middle. "How...?" She couldn't get out anything beyond the single word, one that didn't come close to capturing all the questions bombarding her.

"I asked Pete Kayne how someone would go about finding a birth parent if no one knew who that parent was."

Angel shot to her feet. "Why would you do that?"

She'd spoken so loudly she was aware she'd startled the family. They moved toward the trail to leave.

Hunter looked confused by her outburst. "Because you said you'd like to know about your heritage, for your sake and for Julia's."

"Yes, but it was my decision when and if to pursue

that." He'd gone behind her back, and with something so personal? He'd kept it from her until springing the big surprise? She spun and walked over to the edge of the overlook, gripping the top rail of the fence there to protect visitors from slipping off the edge.

Several seconds passed before she heard Hunter approach her slowly. To his credit, he didn't try to touch her.

"I'm sorry," he said. "I remembered you saying that sometimes you wished the decision would be made for you so you didn't have to wrestle with it. I thought maybe you needed help taking the first step, like I did asking you out."

"It's not the same thing."

"No, it's not. I'm sorry." Damn, he sounded like a scolded dog might if it could talk. But he was the one in the wrong here.

"I can't believe you talked to Pete about me."

"I didn't. I asked him a generic question. I never mentioned you."

"You should have known he'd assume it was about me. Why else would you ask about such a thing when everyone knows you're not adopted?"

"I just wanted to help, that's all."

"I didn't ask for your help." She realized that sounded harsh, but this was the absolute last thing she'd imagined happening on their day together. "Listen, I understand that you thought you were helping, but I don't tend to like big surprises like this, no matter what I said. They never work out well for me."

"It's just a name. I didn't contact her. You can do that or you can burn it."

Angel jerked at his response. He hadn't exactly raised

his voice, but he didn't sound pleased, either. She took a deep breath and tried to look at the situation from his point of view. He'd given her what he probably considered a gift, one she'd inadvertently led him to believe she might appreciate, and she'd basically thrown it back in his face. Still, this wasn't a necklace or a bottle of perfume or even a lottery ticket. He'd given her something that could take her one step closer to finding out who she really was, and she still had conflicted feelings about whether that was a good idea.

Did she want to find the woman who'd abandoned her? Did she want to hear some excuse about why she'd done so? His gift would force her to make a decision about if she wanted to pursue the truth or not. Before, she could easily avoid it because she had no clue where to start, but Hunter had illuminated the first step on the path. Now she had to decide whether to follow that path or turn her back on it.

"We should get back," Hunter said and turned toward the trail without making eye contact with her.

Without thinking, she reached out and gripped his arm. His gaze didn't immediately meet hers, but after a few seconds of her looking at that profile she loved so much, he made eye contact.

"I'm not mad." Okay, she was a little mad, but the thought of fighting with Hunter made her stomach twist and her heart hurt.

He gave her a little sad smile. "It's kind of you to say that, even though it's not true." He shook his head and shifted his gaze toward the trail. "I told you I wasn't very good at this dating thing."

What was he saying? Was he pulling away at the first sign of conflict?

"Don't you dare do that."

He looked at her again. "What?"

"Pull away. Just because I'm upset doesn't mean I don't want to be with you. I'm not the one who throws people away. I'm the one who gets thrown away."

Her voice broke as she spoke the truth that she'd carried deep inside her every single day of her life, the fear that at any point she could be abandoned again, kicked out of her adoptive family, tossed aside by friends, hated by her daughter, laughed at by the photography world. The logical part of her brain knew she was being ridiculous because there had been no evidence of any of those things happening, and yet it was wedged so deep into the core of her being that she couldn't seem to shake the fear. She'd even dreamed of Hunter laughing in her face as he turned his back on her and walked away while she reached out toward him and sobbed. The fact that the dream hadn't made her walk away from him first out of a sense of self-preservation told her how much he'd come to mean to her. And how vulnerable she was now that the thought of losing him threatened to crush her.

Had she made a huge mistake, yet again, in allowing herself to care so much? But damn it, he'd made it so easy. Even now, when she was upset about his going behind her back, she wanted to pull him into her arms and kiss him silly.

Hunter's expression changed as he turned toward her and placed his hands against the sides of her face. "I would never throw you away. Never."

She wanted to believe him, she really did, but her history kept demanding she remember that what someone said didn't always match what they did. Sometimes they could claim to care about you and still walk away.

* * *

Hunter rode slowly across the pasture, wishing his dad was still around to impart some wisdom about women. Because Angel's reaction to his gift had thrown him for a loop.

He reined to a stop and took off his hat to wipe the sweat away from his forehead. A scan of his surroundings showed that the recent rain had given the place new life. The cattle munched the fresh vegetation, not paying him any mind.

After putting his hat back on, he took a deep breath and wondered what Angel was doing in that moment. They hadn't talked in the couple of days since their trek to the overlook. Though he'd meant well, he realized he'd overstepped. It hadn't been his intention. He hadn't even asked Pete to dig around for specifics having to do with Angel. He'd done that on his own, also thinking he was helping.

Since he and Angel had parted ways after they'd returned to where he'd picked her up in town, Hunter had done his best to put himself in her shoes. How would he feel if his mother had abandoned him, leaving him with no connection to his real identity? Would he want that connection or would he harbor a good-riddance attitude toward the person who'd borne him? He couldn't answer that question because he couldn't imagine it. And maybe that was the problem. He couldn't truly put himself in Angel's shoes or understand how she might feel right now.

Although he did understand the feeling of utter frustration when decisions were made that affected his life but over which he had no control. His father's death and his mother's diagnosis were prime examples of that.

The ringing of his phone broke the silence. His immediate thought was that it was his mom, that he might have to race back to the house because she needed him. But when he saw Angel's name on the display, his heart leaped in an entirely different way. She wouldn't call to tell him she never wanted to see him again, would she?

"Hey," he said in answer.

"I need you to tell me this is a good idea."

Okay, not how he expected the conversation to start, but at least they were talking.

"That depends on what 'this' is."

"Taking the first step toward finding out who I really am."

"You're going to call the nurse?" Maybe what he'd done had been the right thing after all, despite her initial reaction.

"Already did. I'm sitting outside her house, trying to decide whether to go knock on her door or drive away and pretend I never knew she existed."

He tried to think of the best thing to say so that whatever it was would seem like her idea.

"You're already there, so maybe that's your answer."

She sighed. "I'm scared."

"No matter what happens, your family will be there for you." He paused. "So will I. You're a strong woman. You can do this."

He wished he was there to hold her hand, to give her any extra strength she might need. But he wondered if it was better he wasn't, if this might be something she had to do on her own.

"Thank you."

"No need to thank me. I hope you get the answers you need."

"Okay, I'm going in."

"Call me later?"

"Okay." And then she was gone.

Hunter looked up at the wide blue sky and prayed that this meeting would be a positive step for Angel, that he hadn't led her to even more heartbreak in an ill-advised attempt to give her something meaningful to show how much he cared about her.

Loved her.

So many times he'd wanted to tell her, but he'd refrained by telling himself it was too much, too early. After finally being with her, he didn't want to scare her away. He could wait to say the words, but in the meantime he'd show her with actions so that when he finally did tell her she'd believe him.

Angel had heard the expression countless times, but was it possible for a person's heart to literally pound out of her chest? Because hers was so loud that she barely heard herself knock on Camille Worth's front door. Not for the first time, she wished she hadn't come alone. She hadn't told anyone in her family where she was going, not even that she was in possession of Camille's name and contact information. She didn't want to have to explain if she chickened out, didn't want her parents to think that her search for answers in any way meant they weren't enough for her. It wasn't a maternal relationship she was looking for with this meeting, just possibly some answers to questions that had plagued her for as long as she could remember.

She gasped as the door opened to reveal a petite African American woman with beautiful gray hair. Her smile was wide and welcoming, as if Angel had shown up on her doorstep with freshly baked cookies, a basketful of wriggling puppies and a big fat sweepstakes check.

"You must be Angel," Camille said, opening the door wide. "Come in, come in."

"Thank you." Angel stepped across the threshold into the cute little cottage in a quiet Austin neighborhood.

"Can I get you something to drink?"

Angel's instinct was to decline, but honestly her throat was so dry she was afraid she might not be able to hold a conversation.

"Water would be great."

"Coming right up. Sit wherever you like."

Angel walked the rest of the way into the living room and took a seat on the end of the couch. Glancing around the room, she spotted a host of family photos full of smiling people. It wasn't unlike the collection in her own family's living area. Her mom had more framed photos along the fireplace mantel than some people had in their entire homes.

As Camille reentered the room, Angel gestured toward some of the photos. "Looks like you have a big family."

"Not too big," she said. "Just one daughter, and she has two kids. A lot of these," she said, gesturing toward the photographs around the room, "are the babies I helped take care of in the hospital nursery over the years."

"You kept in contact with them?"

"Not all, but quite a few. I worked a lot in the NICU, so I spent a lot of time with babies whose parents couldn't always be there. That's where I met you."

"I was in the NICU?" Her mom had never told her that.

"Only briefly, until you were assessed and found to be remarkably healthy, considering."

Considering she'd been abandoned, it made sense that the doctors and nurses might have expected her mother to have not had good neonatal care and that Angel could have problems.

"Do you know who my mother was?"

Camille gave a sad-looking shake of her head. "I wish I did."

Angel's heart sank. This trip had been for nothing. She'd allowed herself to begin to get her hopes up only to have them crushed. She should have known better.

"I think I saw her outside the hospital, but that was before I even knew you were there."

"Then what made you notice her?"

"She was crying as she ran across the street. I thought maybe someone she loved had died in the hospital or something, but later that day I put two and two together. When I saw this beautiful little baby, I realized the woman I'd seen must be the mother. I remember she had long hair, dark like yours, and it was braided all the way down to her hips. She got into a little beat-up truck that sounded awful when she started it."

"What color was it?"

"Hard to say. It was one of those nondescript colors, like it could have been brown but just as easily been some shade of green."

Angel didn't even ask if she'd seen the license plate. Why would she have even noticed such a thing? And even if she had, it was doubtful she would have remembered after all these years.

"I wish I could give you more information."

"It's okay." Angel forced a smile. "It's more than I had a few minutes ago."

"I know it won't help you find her, but I think the note she left with you was completely honest. She thought she was doing the best thing for you. Nobody cries like that if they don't care."

When Angel left, she was able to drive only out of sight of Camille's house before she had to pull over. Camille had been convinced that her birth mother had loved her. Could she trust that assessment? After all, Camille wasn't a young woman anymore. She could be misremembering the events of that day. Angel had more information now, but she didn't have a clue what to do with it.

She leaned her head back and took several deep breaths, trying to calm down and discern her next step.

Hunter's face popped to mind, and in the next moment she was pulling back out onto the street and heading toward Blue Falls. She might not know what she was going to do with the fragments of her past she'd uncovered, but she knew without a doubt she wanted to see Hunter. Maybe he had the answers that escaped her.

Chapter 11

Hunter had just finished reconciling the bank records when he heard a vehicle coming up the driveway. Even before his mom called out from the front porch to let him know Angel was there, he'd known it was her. He couldn't escape the feeling that the next few minutes were going to make or break his relationship with her.

By the time he closed down the computer and walked out onto the porch, Angel was already out of her truck and halfway to the house. He couldn't tell what the expression she wore meant, so he descended the steps.

"Be back in a bit, Mom."

"Take your time."

Neither he nor Angel said anything until they were inside the barn, out of sight and earshot of where his mom sat.

"Are you okay?" he asked as he turned to face Angel.

She nodded, then proceeded to tell him about her meeting with Camille. "I feel like I'm trying to put together a puzzle but all I have are three pieces of one corner."

"You want to dig more and find your mom?" He wasn't going to make any more assumptions without asking her first.

She didn't immediately answer. Instead, she fiddled with one of the buttons on the front of his shirt, and he had to push away the image of her unbuttoning them slowly as she held his gaze. Now wasn't the time and this wasn't the place for those kinds of thoughts.

"I don't think there's any going back now, but I'm scared of what I might find."

He placed one hand atop her shoulder and used his other to lift her chin so that her gaze met his. "You don't have to do it alone."

"I know."

He lowered his mouth to hers, and this time he didn't let them get carried away. Instead, it was a kiss of support. One that showed how much she meant to him without words.

His mom convinced Angel to stay for dinner, and Angel revealed her search for her birth mother and how she was stuck as to where to turn next. To his surprise, it was his mom who offered an avenue that had occurred to neither him nor Angel.

"Chances are your mother didn't drive for days to get here. She was probably either from Texas or one of the surrounding states. Why don't you contact the authorities for the various tribes and see if anyone remembers someone being pregnant at the right time but then not having a baby afterward?"

"Wouldn't that have sent up red flags? I doubt she would have gone back where she came from," Angel said.

Hunter gripped her hand in his. "It can't hurt, and you have to start somewhere."

Angel appeared to consider that for a moment before nodding once. "You're right."

Not caring that his mom was sitting across the table, he lifted Angel's hand to his lips and kissed her fingers. The smile that brought to her face filled him with a lightness that made him realize he'd do anything for this woman, anything to make her happy, make her life easier, to keep her from harm. Because he loved her like he'd never loved anyone before.

Angel thought she might throw up. It had been a month since she'd started contacting officials of tribes or for counties where there was a significant Native population in Texas, Louisiana and Oklahoma with next to no response. So when a member of the Choctaw Nation in Oklahoma had called her, it had taken her a few seconds to realize what was happening.

"Honey, are you okay?"

Angel's head spun a bit as she looked up at the worried expression on her mom's face. Luckily, Julia was spending the day at the house of a friend who had a pool.

"Is something wrong with Julia?" her mother asked, fear evident in her voice.

Angel managed to shake her head. "No, it's not that."

Her mom set aside the basket of vegetables she'd just picked from the garden and came to sit in the rocking chair next to Angel's on the front porch. "Then why do you look as if all the blood has drained out of your face?"

There was no more holding off on telling her family the truth. "I've been searching for my birth mother, and I think I might have found her."

"Oh." It was her mom's turn to look stunned.

"Please don't be upset," Angel said. "This doesn't mean anything bad about you and Dad. You know I couldn't love you more if you were my biological parents."

"It's not that, honey. I just don't want you to get hurt again."

"I know. And trust me, I've thought about that a lot. It's why I've held off so long, why I didn't know if I'd ever try to find her."

"But something changed. This is about Julia's family tree project, isn't it?"

"Partially. But…I guess I just need answers, to know who I am. I want to know why she didn't keep me." She'd mulled the reasons over and over and over again, and a voice had become more insistent lately that she needed to put her past to rest so she could fully embrace her future. A future that she hoped always included Hunter.

They'd spent as much time as they could together over the past month. He'd helped her with her search, given her strength when she'd faltered and kissed her more times than she could count. And as if he hadn't stolen enough of her heart, he'd been more of a father to Julia than Dave ever could have been. Her whole family loved him and his mom. He'd sat beside his mother as Arden had interviewed her for an intimate piece on what it was like living with Alzheimer's disease, helped out Sloane with her latest ranch camp and taken part in more than one poker game with Angel's dad and brothers.

Neither she nor Hunter had professed their love yet, but she believed deep down that they were in love. Maybe he didn't want to push her, and she still struggled sometimes with the fear of losing him, that one day he'd wake up and realize she was lacking in some way and decide he didn't want her.

"Then I think you should find her," her mom said, drawing Angel out of her wandering thoughts.

"You won't be upset? What about Dad?"

"Don't worry about us. We know you love us, and we love you enough to understand that you deserve whatever answers you seek."

Tears pooled in Angel's eyes. "You are the best mom anyone could ever ask for."

"I am pretty awesome, aren't I?"

Angel laughed, grateful for her mom's sense of humor. "I guess I should make plans for a trip to Oklahoma."

"You shouldn't go alone. Take Hunter with you."

"I'd love that, but he can't leave his mom for that long."

"Don't worry about Evelyn. She can stay here. Julia will love that."

Angel jumped up and wrapped her mom in a hug. "I love you, Mom."

"I love you more."

Angel stepped off the porch and walked along the road that led to the pasture as she pulled out her phone and called Hunter.

"Hey, beautiful," he said in greeting, making her smile ear to ear.

"How would you feel about taking a trip?"

Angel sank onto the edge of the bed at the Choctaw Motor Lodge, not sure what was occupying more space in her brain—the fact that she might this very day come face-to-face with her birth mother or that the room she would be sharing with Hunter had a single bed. Hunter had agreed to let her pay for the room if they got only one. Knowing he wasn't flush with funds, she'd booked the single room available thanks to a big festival and powwow that was going on this weekend. Though the front desk clerk had told her the room had two double beds, she'd opened the door to find a king instead.

She couldn't deny she liked the idea of sharing the bed with Hunter, but she was such an emotional mess that she didn't think she was going to be in a romantic frame of mind. Plus, would Hunter think she'd deliberately booked a room with only one bed? She supposed she'd find out when he returned from the fast-food place across the street with their lunch.

With the door open so he'd know which room to return to, she could hear the sounds of air-conditioning units struggling to keep up with the summer heat, the passing of cars on the street and the distant sound of drums that must be coming from the fairgrounds where the powwow was being held. Was her mother there even now? Had the woman she'd talked to decided to tell Angel's birth mother about her inquiries? Would that knowledge make her mother run yet again?

Angel shook her head. She had to stop thinking about her as her mother. There was just as much chance that she wasn't, that this was a wasted trip. Sure, the circumstances all seemed to fit, but she couldn't let herself get her hopes up too high. Even if this Nora Martin was the woman who'd given birth to her, there was no guarantee she was a good or likable person. Angel had run so many scenarios through her mind that her brain was exhausted from the effort.

She looked up at the sound of footsteps outside the door just in time to see Hunter pause before stepping in.

He glanced at the bed but didn't comment as he placed the bags of food on the small table next to the wall unit pumping out slightly musty chilled air.

"It's not the Ritz, but it'll do," she said as she stood, purposefully moved away from the bed and shut the door.

"I don't need anything fancy."

"Good thing since this was literally the only room available in town." Not that any of the other hotels they'd seen were likely to approach four stars, either, but as long as the room was clean and safe she didn't care. It wasn't as if she was here on vacation.

She sank onto the chair opposite Hunter and accepted the burger he handed her. But when she opened the wrapper, she couldn't make herself take a bite despite the fact she'd not eaten anything all day and it was now midafternoon.

"I know you're anxious, but you need to eat," Hunter said.

"I'm not hungry."

"You still need something in your stomach," he said. "The last thing you want to do when you meet this woman is pass out."

She smiled as much as she could, which wasn't much. "One of these days you're going to need to stop making so much sense all the time."

He grinned. "I'll do my best."

Somehow she managed to force the burger down, but her fries remained untouched. When she saw that Hunter had mowed through his, she pushed her container toward him. Evidently satisfied that she'd at least eaten the burger, he made quick work of her fries, as well.

After they finished eating and Hunter had thrown their trash away, he extended his hand to her.

"You ready?"

She shook her head. "Not even close. A very big part of me wants to go back home and forget I ever came here."

"You'll always wonder, for the rest of your life, if you don't at least meet her."

"What if it's not even her?"

"Then we'll keep looking until we do find her."

She liked how he said "we'll," showing that no matter what today held in store for her, she wasn't alone.

"Thank you for coming with me."

"You've already thanked me at least half a dozen times."

"I know, but it bears repeating. You have a lot on your plate already. You didn't need to take on this, too."

Hunter pulled her to her feet and into his arms. "You should know by now that I'll do whatever's necessary to make you happy."

It wasn't a declaration of love, but to her ears it sounded much the same. Especially combined with the feeling of his arms holding her and the sincerity she saw in his eyes. She wrapped her arms more fully around him and listened to his heartbeat next to her ear. But she resisted the urge to stay right there, avoiding the truth she'd come here to find, and stepped out of his embrace.

"I suppose this isn't going to get any easier."

He ran his thumb across her cheek. "Nope, but I'll be right there beside you."

Hunter drove them to the fairgrounds, and the hotel occupancy rates hadn't lied. Judging by the number of cars parked in seemingly every spot available, it appeared that half the state of Oklahoma had come out for the powwow. Angel didn't know whether to be nervous that there would be so many potential witnesses if things went bad or thankful for such a large crowd she could disappear into.

Angel stared out the windshield of the truck from the passenger seat after Hunter squeezed into a spot and turned off the engine. She slapped her palms against her legs and took a deep breath.

"Well, here goes nothing, I guess." Still, she didn't get out of the truck, not until Hunter came around and opened her door, removing one more obstacle between her and possibly the answers to questions she'd harbored her entire life.

As she stepped out onto unsteady feet, Hunter kissed her on the forehead. "You've got this."

She slipped her hand into his and they wove their way through the field full of vehicles toward the grouping of concession trailers and tents. Abigail, the woman who had contacted her, claimed that Nora would be working at the tent where they were frying and selling funnel cakes. As they moved closer, the knots in Angel's stomach tightened even more. When she smelled the distinctive aroma of fresh funnel cake, she halted.

"You okay?" Hunter asked, concern evident in his tone.

Angel wondered if she wore the same look her mom had seen that day on the front porch when she'd first heard from Abigail. After a couple of seconds she nodded and forced herself to put one foot forward, then another, as if teaching her brain how to walk again.

When they drew close to the tent, she considered the best way to introduce herself. While she ran through possibilities in her head, she stepped into the line of people waiting to buy a funnel cake. Normally, she was a great fan of the fried dough concoction, but today the smell nauseated her.

Hunter took up the spot in line behind her and placed his strong, supportive hands on her shoulders. Even though she knew it was all mental, she felt as if she were literally drawing strength into her body from his. For a fleeting moment, her thoughts drifted back to their hotel room and its single bed, what could possibly happen between them in that bed. But then the line in front of her moved forward, bringing her firmly back to the present and the fact that she might literally be taking one more step toward her birth mother.

She scanned the half-dozen women moving about beneath the tent pouring dough into the grease vat, shaking generous doses of powdered sugar onto the finished products, taking money and making change. Angel couldn't see their faces well from where she stood, couldn't hear if they called each other by name. Which one was Nora? Was she even here? And if she was, how would she greet the questions bubbling in the cauldron of Angel's insides?

Before she was ready, Angel found herself at the front of the line.

"How many?"

"Is Nora Martin here?"

Angel noticed a woman turn away from the fryer, a paper plate bearing a piping hot funnel cake in each hand—both of which she promptly dropped. The wide-eyed look on the woman's face telegraphed the truth even before she lifted a hand to her mouth and started crying.

"Nora, are you okay?" the woman in front of Angel asked.

"I need a minute." Nora's voice was barely above a whisper and almost lost in the noise of other conversations, the sizzle of the fryer and the jingles on the dresses of the female dancers currently performing in the arena.

Angel stepped out of the line, and Hunter's hand slipped down to capture hers. She was probably gripping his so hard that she was cutting off his circulation, but he didn't seem to mind. Nora kept her gaze on Angel the entire time as she skirted the tables lining the outside of the tent until she came face-to-face with Angel, as if she thought she might disappear if she looked away. Ironic.

"Are you really here?" Nora asked.

When she lifted her hand, as if she might touch Angel's face, Angel took a step backward. Nora's hand went to her own cheek instead and wiped away some of her tears.

"You look just like me when I was young." Her expression did appear as if she was looking in a mirror back in time at her younger self.

"Why did you abandon me?" Every way Angel had thought of to introduce herself flew away as the most pressing question shot from her like a cannonball.

Nora's lower lip quivered, and Hunter tugged on Angel's hand.

"Maybe we should go somewhere else to talk," he said, making her aware of all the pairs of eyes staring at them.

"My house isn't far from here," Nora said.

Angel considered the wisdom of letting Nora have the equivalent of home-court advantage, but then she already did, didn't she? So she gave a quick nod.

While Nora went to grab her purse from the tent and tell her coworkers she was leaving, Angel imagined them all asking what was going on. Would she tell them that Angel was the daughter she'd abandoned as a newborn in an entirely different state? How many of them would be shocked? Or did at least some of them know?

Hunter wrapped his arm around Angel's shoulders. "You've already taken the hardest step. You'll get through this."

She kept telling herself that as they followed Nora's dust-covered compact car through a series of streets before she pulled up in front of a small but neat house. It wasn't going to appear in any home magazines, but Nora had planted a bright array of flowers along the front and painted the mailbox a vibrant turquoise blue, Angel's favorite color. Honestly, those splashes of color looked like obvious attempts to add some life to the drabness of the house and lot.

Angel deliberately didn't touch Hunter as they made their way to the front door after Nora. She needed to prove to herself she was strong enough to walk toward the answers she wanted without aid. Sure, Hunter was still close enough she imagined she felt the heat coming off his very masculine body, but the lack of physical connection was something she needed at the moment. She didn't want anything to distract her from the task at hand.

After Nora stepped across the threshold into her home, Hunter touched Angel's shoulder.

"Would you like me to stay outside so you can talk in private?"

She was already shaking her head before he finished his question. Sure, she wanted to prove to herself she could do this on her own, but that didn't mean she wouldn't benefit from the ample amount of moral support he offered by simply being there.

When they stepped inside, Nora indicated a tiny living room that would fit into the one back at the ranch twice over. The furniture was not anywhere near new, and it showed obvious signs of wear. But even a single drive through town had revealed that this slice of Oklahoma was not wealthy. The large plant on the outskirts of town that was being overtaken by scraggly weeds was evidence of a town in decline. She wondered how Nora made a living or if perhaps she had to depend on government assistance as so many people in dying towns left without other viable options often did.

"I'll get us something to drink," Nora said as she stepped to the wide doorway that led into a bright yellow kitchen. She didn't ask what they wanted and Angel wondered if that was because there was only a single option. But she returned with a tray with not only bottles of water but also a couple of soda options.

Considering how little Angel had slept in the past few days, she immediately chose one of the sodas for a quick infusion of caffeine. She and Hunter sat side by side on the couch while Nora sank into one of those cushy chairs that not only rocked but also swiveled. Angel watched as the woman who was a complete stranger to her took a long drink of water. If she wasn't mistaken, she saw Nora's hand shake. After a few seconds of silence, she looked up and met Angel's gaze.

"I don't even know your name."

"Angel."

Nora's hand lifted to her chest. "They kept the name I gave you."

Angel nodded, thinking about the note that had been with her when the hospital staff found her, how that note was sitting in the bottom of her jewelry box even now.

"I left you at that hospital to protect you," Nora said just as suddenly as Angel had asked her the question that precipitated the answer.

"From?" Angel knew she still sounded confrontational, making her acutely aware of all the anger she'd long buried deep inside.

Nora looked up and met Angel's gaze. "Your father. He was a violent man. He used to beat me, even when I was pregnant with you, but I managed to always protect you from his fists." Nora took a shaky breath. "But I was afraid that after you were born, I wouldn't be able to and so I took off. It nearly killed me to leave you behind, but I knew it was the right thing to do. It was the only way you were going to have a chance in life. Not a day has gone by since that I haven't wondered about you, hoped that you ended up with a good family who loved you."

Angel saw the question in Nora's eyes, and part of her didn't want to answer. But there was such raw emotion staring back at her. Coupled with what Camille had told her about seeing Nora sobbing as she ran from the hospital, Angel found herself believing Nora, wanting to alleviate some of that old pain despite how much it had caused Angel.

"I did. My parents are wonderful."

Nora bit her lip, and Angel saw the shimmer of unshed tears in the woman's eyes. "Thank the Lord. Do you have brothers and sisters?"

Angel nodded. "Three brothers and a sister, all adopted."

"That's wonderful."

Suddenly, another question formed in Angel's mind,

demanding to be answered. Did she have more brothers and sisters, ones who shared her blood? "Did you have other children?"

Sadness clouded Nora's expression. "No. As soon as I could, I had a hysterectomy so there was no chance I'd ever get pregnant again."

Angel jerked at that answer, evidently enough that Nora noticed.

"Not because of you. I just knew I couldn't go through giving away another child, and there was no way I could raise a child in this house."

Angel's hands curled into fists until she forced herself to relax them. "If he beat you, why would you come back?"

"I had nowhere else to go, no education, no money. I used what I'd taken from Joe's wallet to pay for gas and a little bit of food when I fled to Austin. I barely had enough to get back." She flinched at a memory, and Angel realized that she must not have had a pleasant homecoming. "Plus, at the time my mother was still alive and needed me to help take care of her."

"Didn't everyone wonder why you came back no longer pregnant but with no baby?"

"I told everyone I lost the baby. Some might have suspected otherwise, but no one ever questioned it. I think there were many who didn't blame me for whatever I'd done considering the alternative."

"So my father didn't want me, either?"

Hunter's hand wrapped around hers, giving support but maybe also suggesting she go a bit more easily. As she watched Nora, she wondered if her birth mother was going to answer this time. She picked at the frayed arm of her chair and appeared to be waging a debate in her head. Eventually, she sighed.

"The truth isn't pretty."

"But I want to hear it. I've spent a life with so many questions, so I deserve the answers, no matter what they are."

"Joe didn't ask what happened or where you were. He was just glad not to have another mouth to feed, and then he smacked me so hard for taking the money that I fell into the wall and ended up with a black eye."

Angel couldn't sit still anymore. She stood and paced halfway across the room. Anger toward Nora still sat heavy in her chest, but the more she learned the more she began to understand what kind of home she could have been born into. She, too, might have followed a similar path of abuse.

"Is he going to walk in here any minute?"

"I hope not. He died three years ago. Lung cancer."

Despite all she'd learned about Joe Martin, Angel experienced what felt like a punch to her lungs. She would never meet the man who'd been her birth father. As she stood there in the middle of Nora's living room absorbing the news, she realized that perhaps that was for the best. He didn't sound like anyone she'd ever want to know. Honestly, she was still undecided about Nora.

Chapter 12

Hunter didn't know if he'd ever seen someone appear so wrung out and exhausted before. Angel looked not only physically tired but also as if her brain might need to hibernate for a while, as well. He reached across the cab of the truck as he stopped at a red light and took her hand.

"You okay?"

"I think so, though I feel as if I could sleep for a week and still not be rested."

That was understandable considering she'd just spent several hours questioning her birth mother about Nora's life, Nora's decision to abandon Angel instead of putting her officially up for adoption and her Choctaw heritage. And Nora seemed to soak up every piece of information Angel shared about her own life as if she'd been starving for it ever since she'd run away from the hospital all those years ago. Maybe she had.

When Nora found out she had a granddaughter, she'd begun to cry. Angel had showed her a picture of Julia on her phone, and the tears had streamed down Nora's cheeks.

She's so beautiful, Nora had said, and then her crying had turned into full-blown sobbing.

Hunter and Angel had exchanged glances, neither knowing the right way to respond. And then Angel had taken a huge step when she reached out and wrapped her hand around Nora's.

I'm sorry, Nora had said through her sobs. *I'm so, so sorry.*

That broke something inside Angel, and she'd begun to cry, too. And he'd felt utterly helpless. So he'd stepped out onto the porch to give them a few minutes of privacy to let out the raw emotion and collect themselves. By then the sun had sunk below the horizon and he could see the first few stars in the sky. After several minutes, Angel came out to say that Nora had invited them to stay for dinner. And so they'd ended up sitting around Nora's little Formica-topped table, eating chicken-fried steak with mashed potatoes, hominy and *banaha*, a Choctaw bread.

Nora had seemed more relaxed at the table, and she'd even asked him about himself and his family. She sympathized when he told her about his mom's diagnosis, sharing that she worked in a nursing home and had seen how the disease could steal who a person had always been. She'd realized then what she'd said and apologized, but he'd responded that there was no need because he'd read enough to know what was coming.

Now, as he drove back to the hotel, he thought about those facts again, how he had pushed away the truth over the past few weeks as he and Angel had grown closer. The doubt came back. Was it incredibly selfish of him to get more involved with her when the years ahead were going to require that his attention be on his mother? She would gradually need more and more help, and he had no idea how he was going to handle it while also working enough to keep a roof over their heads and food on the table. An unusual feeling of panic clawed its way up his chest, causing his heart to speed up. He took a deep breath to calm down. He'd figure things out when the time came.

"What's wrong?"

He glanced over at Angel. "I'm just wiped, too."

Despite being dog tired, when they reached their room his gaze took in the king-size bed again. He'd forced himself not to think about it earlier, how he was going to be sleeping next to the woman who'd come to mean more to him than even he could have imagined after all the years of crushing on her. His body stirred at the thought of how they might make use of that bed, but now was not the time. Angel needed sleep, and a lot of it.

"I think I'll take a shower," he said, aiming to give her time to change and pick the side of the bed she preferred. If he kept thinking about Angel in that bed, he was going to have to do more in the bathroom than shower.

He took his time, not wanting to rush Angel. But when he came out, she wasn't curled up asleep as he'd expected. Instead, she sat motionless on the side of the bed in the same clothes she'd been wearing all day.

"Angel?"

She lifted her gaze slowly to his. "Have you ever had so much going on in your head that it felt impossible to ever sleep again, no matter how tired you were?"

He crossed to the bed and sat down beside her. "Yeah, the night after Mom was diagnosed with Alzheimer's disease. It felt like my brain was some combination of a race car and a Ping-Pong ball."

"That sounds about right." She leaned her head against his shoulder.

"Why don't you go take a warm shower? Maybe that will relax you enough so that you can sleep."

"I don't think I could stand up that long." But she did stand and retrieve some clothes from her suitcase and head for the bathroom.

Was she so tired that she was saying one thing but doing another?

Though he normally slept in just his underwear, he kept on the pair of shorts and T-shirt he was wearing and stretched out on the opposite side of the bed, giving her plenty of room so that she didn't feel crowded. His head had just hit the pillow when she came back out wearing a thin T-shirt and pajama shorts that exposed the length of her gorgeous legs. Hunter was thankful he was already under the cover, though he did shift onto his side so that he didn't obviously tent it.

He expected her to curl up on the other edge of the bed and fall immediately to sleep. Instead, she slipped under the cover and all the way across the bed to him.

"Angel?"

She didn't say anything in response. Instead, she lifted her mouth to his and kissed him like a sweetheart welcoming home a soldier after a long deployment. When her tongue slid into his mouth, his entire body was flooded with heat and lust. He wanted this woman like he'd never wanted anything or anyone in his life. But he somehow cobbled together enough sense to pull away.

"You're so tired you're not thinking straight." His body screamed in protest that he was denying what she was offering.

He jerked when her hand slipped underneath his shirt and started making its way up over his chest.

"Yes, I'm tired, but not so tired that I don't know what I want."

"Just a few minutes ago you said you were so exhausted that you couldn't even stand in the shower."

"This doesn't require standing."

He closed his eyes and ran a hand over his face. "You're trying to kill me, aren't you?"

When she didn't answer, he opened his eyes and examined the look on her face. His heart hurt at how rejected she appeared to be. He lifted his hand to her face and caressed her gently.

"It's not that I don't want to. Heaven knows I do. But I don't want you to do this because of the circumstances," he said, gesturing to the bed, "or because you've got all these emotions twisting inside you."

Angel placed two fingers against his lips. "Stop." She let her fingertips run lightly over his cheek. "I can't tell you how many times I've fantasized about this because I've lost count. We've just never had this kind of opportunity."

She was right. They were always around other people, or had family responsibilities tugging them in opposite directions.

"It's been a hell of a day," she said. "I want it to end with us together. Really together."

"If you're sure." *Oh, please be sure.*

She lifted away from him, and he nearly groaned in pain. He'd talked her out of what he, too, had done a hell of a lot of fantasizing about. But when she grabbed the hem of her shirt and lifted it over her head, leaving her breasts bare and on full display, he took her at her word and rolled her onto her back.

They alternated kissing and getting rid of the rest of their clothes. When they were naked, skin on heated skin, he had to take a deep breath or he would really embarrass himself.

Angel placed her palm against his cheek. "It's been a long time for me, too."

"I don't want to ruin this."

She smiled at him. "You won't."

She sounded so confident, and he really, really hoped this wasn't just the most vivid dream he'd ever had about her. That would be cruelty at the highest level. And he hoped that she wasn't disappointed afterward, especially considering her past with men. He felt enormous honor and responsibility that she'd chosen to be with him, to trust him when it wasn't easy for her to trust.

He ran his hand gently over her silky hair. "You're so beautiful."

She reached up and wrapped her hand around his neck, pulling him down to her for another kiss that rocked his world. The way their hands ran over each other's bodies, coaxing moans of pleasure and the desire for even more, grew more heated and insistent. Somehow he managed to remember the condoms he'd stashed in his bag just in case.

"You're certain?" he asked against her ear.

"Yes," she said in a breathy voice that sent him bolting for the protection as fast as he could.

Angel couldn't move. If the hotel caught fire around her, she was fairly certain she'd burn. That was what happened when you've just had the best sex of your life, sex so awesome that everything that had come before seemed like only an imposter instead of the real thing.

Beside her, Hunter lay on his back, still trying to bring his breathing back to normal, same as her.

"You okay?" he asked, also without moving.

"I think the word you're looking for is *fabulous*."

He chuckled and somehow found the energy to roll onto his side to look at her. "That right?"

"How would you describe it?"

"A dream come true. Literally."

She glanced over at him. "Really?"

"Yep. Only the dreams pale in comparison."

More heat suffused her already overheated body. A part of her mind told her she should be embarrassed, that she should pull a sheet up to cover her breasts, but she didn't want to. Though she would have never thought it of herself, she didn't mind Hunter looking at her naked body. And she certainly liked looking at his.

Hunter let his fingertips trail across the swell of her breasts, and she felt desire stir again. How was that possible when moments before she'd been convinced she was completely sated?

"It's kind of crazy, isn't it, how we've known each other all these years but had no idea we could be like this together?"

"I had some idea," he said, then lowered his mouth to lightly kiss her breast.

"So I'm the only one who was clueless?"

"To be fair, I didn't know *how* great this would be."

"So it was good for you, too?"

"I'd think that was obvious." He ran his hand down

her side and let it rest where her waist and hip met. "I don't ever want to leave this bed."

That sounded glorious.

"But you were exhausted even before," he said. "We should get some sleep."

"Sleep is overrated."

He laughed. "Where did you get this second wind, woman? Because I'd like one."

Angel wished they didn't have to stop exploring each other's bodies and bringing each other pleasure like she'd never known before, but after making love again she couldn't keep her eyes open. As Hunter pulled her close to his side and covered them both, she drifted toward sleep feeling happier than she'd ever thought possible.

Hunter came awake with a jolt, disoriented for several seconds until he remembered where he was and realized that his phone was ringing. Beside him, Angel sat up suddenly, concern on her face that mirrored what slammed into him. No one would call this early unless something was wrong. Light was barely coming in from around the curtains when he managed to grab the phone.

"Hello," he said, his voice still heavy with sleep.

"Hunter, it's Diane." He tried not to react to the fact that Diane was calling him instead of Angel.

"Who is it?" Angel asked in a whisper.

He held up a finger. "Is everything okay?"

"It is now, but we had a bit of a scare last night. I thought you should know, your mom woke up and didn't know where she was. She walked through the house calling out for you, and when Julia came out of her room, well…she grabbed her and shook her a bit, asking where you were."

Hunter's heart sank, and he hated himself for leaving his mother alone, depending on others to watch out for her when it was his responsibility.

"Are they okay?"

Beside him, Angel stiffened. "What happened?" She didn't whisper this time.

"Is Angel there?"

"Yes, ma'am. Are they okay?" he asked again. If his mom hurt Julia, she'd never forgive herself. He'd never forgive himself for putting Julia in danger and his mom in the position to hurt someone. But she'd never done anything like that. He felt sick that her disease had chosen when he was away to advance another step.

"Shaken up, but everyone is fine now. Your mom is really embarrassed, though. Hunter, it was like she suddenly woke up from sleepwalking and realized what she was doing. I think she cried the rest of the night."

"We'll be there as soon as we can." He hung up without offering Angel the phone or waiting for a response. They needed to not waste any time getting on the road.

"Hunter, tell me what's wrong," Angel said as she grabbed his arm.

He repeated what her mother had told him while he pulled on the clothes he'd tossed onto the floor last night.

"Is Julia hurt?"

He heard the panic in her voice, and when he looked at her his heart sank. She looked like a mama bear who would attack his mother if she'd injured Julia in any way. He couldn't say he blamed her, but he felt the same protective instinct toward his mom. This whole thing was his fault.

"I'm sorry. I shouldn't have left Mom."

He knew in that moment he'd never be able to leave her in anyone else's care outside her comfort zone again.

Angel felt as if the distance between Oklahoma and Blue Falls grew larger with every mile Hunter drove. Neither of them had said anything for a long while, and when she glanced at him he didn't even look like the man who'd made love to her last night. Gone were the smiles, the looks of pleasure, the happiness. His posture was tense and more than once she saw him force his grip to loosen on the steering wheel.

Of course, she likely looked every bit as tense. She wished they could magically transport home instead of worrying about what they'd find for seemingly endless hours. They should be spending this time waking up in each other's arms, maybe even making love again, then meeting Nora for breakfast before they headed home at a normal pace. As it was, Hunter would be lucky if he didn't get pulled over for speeding. Not that she wanted him to go slower. She needed to hold her daughter in her arms, make sure with her own eyes that she was okay despite the fact that her mother had assured her Julia wasn't harmed beyond being scared and not understanding how Evelyn could be fun one moment and then scary the next.

Guilt swamped her that she'd not been there to comfort her daughter, that she'd been so far away. She couldn't help the thought that if she hadn't started things with Hunter, the whole ordeal would have never happened.

Angel hated that this was happening to Evelyn, that it was breaking Hunter's heart, but Julia was her number one priority. Keeping her safe was her top duty as a mother. If that meant making sure she was never alone with Evelyn, then that was what would have to happen.

She wanted to find something to say to break the silent tension inside the cab of the truck, but what could she say? Small talk wasn't appropriate. It felt wrong to be happy about the amazing night they'd spent together. Actually, it felt as if they were being punished for daring to take some time for themselves.

And she didn't want to delve into the fact that no matter the cause, his mother had grabbed and scared the most important person in Angel's life. The idea that Evelyn could have hurt Julia without meaning to made her stomach twist into painful knots. That fact wasn't going away, and she doubted she'd be able to hide her conflicted feelings about the situation from Evelyn when she saw her. Maybe once she held Julia and made sure with her own eyes that she was fine, she'd relax. But she had a sinking feeling in her middle that Hunter would never relax again.

The miles ticked by in agonizing silence. She hated how she hadn't been able to get enough of Hunter the night before and now it was as if they were strangers forced to take a road trip together. And that she had not the first clue how to regain the closeness they'd shared such a short time ago. Maybe all he needed was to see his mother in person, too, to make sure she was okay, to take her back to where she was comfortable.

When they finally rolled into Blue Falls, it felt as if they'd been gone for ages. So much had happened since they'd left. With her thoughts so preoccupied with getting home to Julia, she hadn't really been able to process the fact that she'd actually met and talked to her birth mother, that they might be able to build some sort of relationship, that her fears that the woman would be horrible had all been for naught.

The truth was that despite the fact Nora could have possibly found help if she'd looked, Angel accepted that Nora had felt trapped with no options other than to give up her baby in a way that would keep her birth father from ever looking for her, putting her in danger. Part of the reason Nora had gone back to her husband was to sell the story that she'd lost their baby, so he'd never know that Angel was out there somewhere. As Nora had divulged all the details, Angel's heart had ached for her. She tried to imagine herself in Nora's shoes, and the truth was she would have done whatever was necessary to protect Julia.

She had no idea what the future held for her relationship with Nora, but she'd have to deal with that later. One life upheaval at a time.

As Hunter pulled into the ranch drive a few minutes later, she gripped the door handle so hard she thought she might leave indentations where her fingers dug in. Though she belatedly thought it might make him feel even worse than he already did about what had happened, she opened the door and hopped out even before he'd turned off the engine. But by the time she made it to the porch, where her mom met her, Hunter was close behind.

"Where's Julia? Is she okay?"

"She's fine, dear. I told you that."

"I need to see her."

"She's out back playing."

"And my mom?" Hunter asked.

There was sympathy written all over her mom's face as she looked up at Hunter. "She was so agitated, wanting to go home, that Mildred came and got her early this morning."

"I'm sorry about this," he said, his voice strained. "It won't happen again."

"Honey, it's unfortunately just part of the disease. Your mom is a sweet soul, and she was mortified by what happened. She apologized profusely, to all of us."

"That's really kind of you to say, but I should have never put you or her in the situation in the first place."

Angel knew her mother well enough to know that if Hunter had been standing closer, she would have reached out and taken his hands in support. But Hunter stood so rigidly that it felt as if he'd erected a thick armor around himself to keep everyone away.

"Don't be so hard on yourself," her mom said. "You deserve a life, too." She shifted her gaze to Angel. "Both of you do."

With that, she went into the house, leaving the two of them alone to say their goodbyes.

"Tell Julia I'm sorry," he said as he turned to leave.

Though she needed to see Julia, she instinctively reached out and gripped his arm. "Hunter, wait."

She didn't want them to part this way, not after what they'd shared the night before. She was in love with him, and she wished with all her heart that she could take away his guilt, his stress, his pain. That she could make his mom completely healthy. But she couldn't, and they'd have to find a way to navigate their reality.

He leaned forward and gave her a quick kiss on the forehead. "I'll call you."

And then he was eating up the distance to his truck with his long strides. She felt as if she'd taken only a single breath before he was speeding down her drive-way. A pool of fear formed in her middle that it was for the final time.

Chapter 13

To look at Julia, you'd never know that she'd been so scared the night before that she'd slept with her grandparents. Now she giggled as she repeatedly tossed a stick for Maggie, her favorite furry companion, to chase. Each time Julia threw the stick, Maggie would bark once, then speed off as if she were being timed in a competition for the world's biggest bag of dog treats.

Angel's panic that her mom might have been keeping part of a scary truth from her dissipated.

Julia smiled and ran toward Angel when she saw her. "Mom, you're home!"

Angel bent down and opened her arms to receive her daughter. "Hey, sweetie. I missed you."

"I missed you, too. Where did you go?"

Without letting on what she was doing, Angel scanned her daughter, looking for any sort of injury but mercifully finding none. "Oklahoma."

"What were you and Hunter doing in Oklahoma?"

Okay, so maybe she should go ahead and tell Julia about everything that had transpired since she'd left. Well, not everything. She wouldn't share everything even if Julia was an adult. Some of it was private, and Angel's face heated at the mere thought of all those hours in bed with Hunter. She missed him already despite the tension that had settled between them since her mom's early phone call.

Angel stood and took Julia's hand, then led her to one of the picnic tables beneath the shade trees. Once they were seated side by side on one of the benches, backs leaning against the table, she tried to figure out how to begin. Maybe just dive in without preamble as she had with Nora.

"I found my birth mother and went to meet her."

Julia looked confused for a moment, but then her eyes widened. "You did?"

Angel nodded. "She lives in a small town in Oklahoma, and her name is Nora. And guess what."

"What?"

"Now I know what our heritage is. We are Choctaw."

"Choctaw," Julia said slowly, as if testing out the feel of the word on her tongue. "How is that different from other tribes?"

"We'll do some research together, okay?"

"Books from the library?"

"Yes, and reading online."

"Is she nice?"

Angel didn't hesitate because, despite her conflicted feelings, she knew the truth. "She is."

"Did you meet your real dad, too?"

"Your grandpa is my real dad, but no. My birth father died a few years ago."

"That's sad."

Angel didn't ever wish death on anyone, but she couldn't agree that it was sad. By Nora's account, he hadn't been a good person, but Julia didn't need to know that, at least not at her young age.

"Why did your mom leave you at that hospital?"

Angel had hoped in vain Julia wouldn't ask that question. "She wasn't able to take care of me."

"Why not?"

Angel sighed. So much for keeping the harsh truth away from her inquisitive daughter. She should have known better.

"My birth father wasn't a nice man, and Nora was afraid he might hurt me."

Julia looked appropriately shocked. "Who would hurt a little baby?"

No one who had an ounce of goodness in them.

"Most people wouldn't, but some people are not like the rest of us. For some reason, they have a lot of anger inside them and they take it out on others by hurting them."

"Like when I wanted to punch Cara for saying bad things about us?"

"Not exactly. Yes, that's anger, and we all feel it sometimes, but not all of us act on it. You were mad, but you didn't punch Cara. That's good. It would have just gotten you in trouble and not changed her mind. Some people don't hold back, though. They don't know how to express what they're feeling except with their fists."

Julia placed her small hand atop Angel's. "I'm glad

Nora gave you to Grandma and Grandpa, but I think she was sad to give up her baby."

Angel recalled how Nora had instantly started to cry the moment she saw her. "She was, but sometimes mothers have to do whatever's necessary to protect their children."

"Can I visit her? I've never been to Oklahoma."

"Maybe. We'll see." Right now, Angel's protective instincts were telling her to keep Julia on the ranch and away from anyone who wasn't a Hartley. That wasn't realistic, but she couldn't help how she felt.

Julia looked back toward the house. "Did Grandma tell you about Evelyn?"

"She did. I'm sorry that scared you. I know Evelyn is sorry, too."

"Why did that happen? Grandma said it's because Evelyn has a disease, the one that makes her forget stuff."

"That's right. I know she'd take it back if she could. Alzheimer's disease makes people do things they'd normally never do."

"Why do people get diseases?"

"I don't know, sweetie. They just do sometimes. It's not fair, but life isn't always fair." Her thoughts drifted to Hunter, who had faced more than his share of unfairness.

"Will you get a disease and forget who I am?"

Angel's heart broke at both the idea of that happening and the fact that Julia would fear such a thing.

"I hope not." She hugged Julia close and kissed the top of her head.

"Can we go see Evelyn to make sure she's okay?"

That Julia would want to do that after Evelyn had scared her the night before spoke to the kindness her child possessed.

"Not today. She needs some time without visitors."

Though Angel had to admit that part of her wished she could be there at Hunter's side to give him support the way he'd been for her the day before. It felt wrong that he had to do this alone. She hoped he knew he could call her at any time, that he would instead of trying to shoulder all the responsibility himself.

"When we do visit, I think we should take Evelyn a cake."

Angel smiled. "That sounds like a great idea."

He knew as soon as he saw the expression on Mildred's face that he wasn't going to like what he found when he stepped inside.

"She's not forgiving herself," Mildred said. "As if she deliberately scared that little girl. I've never seen her like this before."

He heard the sadness in Mildred's voice. She and his mom had been friends for decades, since way before he was born.

"Thank you for going to get her. I'm sorry you had to. I should have been here."

"You stop that right this instant." Mildred's voice was firm and invited no argument. "You cannot put your life on hold for the remainder of your mom's life. God only knows how long that will be. Could be years and years, and you will have wasted the prime of your life."

"She's my responsibility," he said.

"No, she's your mother. You love her, take care of her the best you can, but you don't use her as an excuse to not live your own life."

He appreciated what Mildred was trying to do, but no one could understand the position he was in unless they were in the same situation. It would be different if his dad was still alive or if he had brothers and sisters. But he was all his mom had.

"You want me to stay?" Mildred asked.

He shook his head. "You've already done enough. Go on home."

She pulled him into a hug, and he realized how much she'd been like a second mother to him.

"You remember what I said. There's no need for you to be a martyr."

He made a sound that he hoped came across like agreement, then stepped through the door. The main part of the house was quiet, so he walked toward his mom's room. He found her door closed, so he lightly knocked before opening it.

"Mom?"

He found her lying on her side, staring out the window. She looked so incredibly small and frail like that. Since she'd been diagnosed, he could sometimes forget she was sick because she didn't look ill. But now he saw the toll the disease was taking on her.

Pushing down his sudden urge to cry, something he rarely did, he crossed the room and sat in the comfy chair on the opposite side of her nightstand.

"You should put me in the nursing home," she said, instantly breaking his heart.

"That's not going to happen, ever."

"I might forget who you are and hurt you."

"Mom, don't say things like that. You would never hurt me."

She finally met his gaze. "You don't know that. I've read enough about the disease to know that I'll forget the people closest to me. I'll lash out at the people I love the most."

He scooted to the edge of the chair. "I'm a good eight inches taller than you and outweigh you by probably seventy pounds. Do you really think you could hurt me?"

"I don't want to take that chance."

He knew she must have played last night over and over in her mind a thousand times. "You didn't hurt Julia."

"But I could have. She's *not* bigger than me." She bit her lip when it started to tremble.

"I'm sorry I left you there. That was a mistake on my part. I won't leave you alone again."

"I wasn't alone."

"You know what I mean."

She pressed her eyes closed, and his heart ached that she was probably trying to hold back more tears. "Don't let me ruin your life."

"Mom, stop it," he said, his voice probably too sharp, but he was exhausted, emotionally raw and didn't like the sound of her being pitiful. It wasn't her, and she needed to fight to preserve who she really was for as long as she could. Evelyn Millbrook was not the type of woman who felt sorry for herself. She was the woman who worked hard, loved freely and found the best in any situation, no matter how tough. "You're not ruining my life. If I were the one sick, you'd do whatever you could to take care of me. It's no different when it's me taking care of you."

He didn't know if he was really getting through to her, but she finally nodded and agreed to leave her room, where she'd evidently been ever since Mildred had brought her home. She tried to go to the kitchen to cook, but he instead steered her to the front porch.

"Just sit out here and enjoy the fresh air," he said.

She looked as if she might argue, but something in his expression must have caused her to reconsider. Even though he left her sitting on the porch, he made sure to glance out the window every couple of minutes as he set about making sandwiches and soup for them. He wasn't as talented as his mom in the kitchen and was dog tired to boot, but he wanted her to relax, to hopefully let go of the need for self-flagellation.

Thankful that his neighbors had already taken care of the animals, he spent the rest of the day with his mom, wanting to make up for not being there for her when she had her scariest moment yet. He couldn't help but feel he was the cause of it in the first place. They ate, then went for a walk that thankfully seemed to help calm his mom and finally sat on the front porch enjoying two glasses of lemonade as the sun set.

"How did your trip go?" she asked suddenly, making him wonder if she could tell his thoughts had drifted to Angel.

"Okay."

"Was the woman Angel's birth mother?"

He nodded, then gave a few of the highlights without revealing anything Angel might not want shared.

"You were good to go with her."

"It should have been someone in her family."

"Because of me." Sadness crept into her voice again.

"Because I have too much work to be running off to Oklahoma." No matter how wonderful his night with Angel had been.

Part of him wished it hadn't happened at all because

now he knew what he'd be missing. Because he didn't see how there was any way he could continue the relationship, not after the danger he'd put Julia in by leaving his mom in a place where he should have known she could become easily confused. Not to mention the fact that he was going to have to figure out, by some miracle, a way to make more money so that he could hire some in-home care for her so he could work and not leave her alone. He no longer trusted that the next big advance in her disease might not cause her to wander away from the ranch, potentially into the road, or that she might hurt herself in some way without even leaving the house.

Every single moment of his waking hours was going to be dedicated to taking care of his mom in some way, making sure that she was safe. As much as it made him ache inside, that left no time for dating. No time for love.

Angel wandered into the kitchen still dressed in her pajamas and with hair that looked as if it had been caught in a tornado. She stopped when she saw the chocolate cake sitting on the kitchen table. Her mouth watered.

"What's the special occasion?" she asked her mom, who was standing at the sink washing her cake pans.

"I made it for you to take to Hunter and his mom."

Angel had mentioned to her mom the night before that after giving Hunter three days to get Evelyn settled back at home, she was going to stop by to see how she was. At least that was what she told herself. Of course, it was only part of the truth. The bigger worry was that she hadn't heard from Hunter other than a couple of responses to her texts. She was worried about him every bit as much as his mom, probably more.

"You didn't have to do that."

"I figured it wouldn't hurt to have chocolate cake to pave the way."

So she hadn't done a very good job of hiding her worry about Hunter's lack of communication. "Thanks. Though it's going to be mighty hard to not dig into this before I get there."

The truth was her stomach was too tied up in knots to even think about eating as she drove toward the Millbrooks' ranch an hour later. But when she arrived, it was Mildred who greeted her at the door.

"Hey, Evelyn, Angel is here with a gorgeous chocolate cake," she called back into the house.

Evelyn walked into view, and Angel saw none of the bright, friendly woman who'd played with Julia as if she were a kid herself.

"I hope you don't mind my stopping by." Angel lifted the cake. "Mom made this for you all this morning."

"She shouldn't have done that," Evelyn said.

Mildred stepped back to allow Angel to enter the living room.

"Evelyn, I hope you're not still worried about Julia. She's perfectly fine. In fact, she keeps asking me when she can come visit you again."

"Really?" Evelyn shook her head. "But that's not a good idea. I don't want to take a chance I might actually hurt her next time."

Mildred took the cake from Angel. "I'll go slice some of this for us."

"It's not even lunchtime yet," Evelyn said.

"It's never too early for chocolate cake."

Angel smiled. "That's my life philosophy."

When Mildred disappeared into the kitchen, Angel walked up to Evelyn and took her hands in hers. "I want you to listen and really hear me. I will admit that I was scared when I heard what happened, but there isn't a mark on Julia. And by the time I got home, she was playing in the backyard with Maggie. She was more concerned about you."

"She's such a kindhearted child."

"She is, and I'm thankful for that. And I explained to her that you would never knowingly scare her. You obviously care about her too much to do that. We talked about Alzheimer's disease and how it sometimes makes people do and say things they don't mean."

Evelyn sank onto the arm of a chair. "I feel like such a burden."

"The people we love are never a burden."

"You sound like Hunter."

"Well, that makes sense. He certainly loves you."

Evelyn looked up at Angel. "I think I'm not the only one he loves. And that's what worries me."

Angel couldn't help the jolt that went through her. Did Evelyn think she wasn't good enough for her son? Was this her disease talking?

Evelyn reached out and clasped Angel's hand. "That came out wrong. I just know how Hunter tends to carry the weight of the world on his shoulders. I'm afraid he won't allow time for himself."

The knot of worry that had been slowly growing in Angel's stomach over the past three days doubled in size. She hoped he still didn't blame himself for Julia's scare. Maybe she should have brought Julia with her so he could see with his own eyes that she was back to her happy, life-is-awesome self with no lingering effects.

She wanted to ask where Hunter was, but she figured since Mildred was here with his mom, he must be working. He could be on the far side of the ranch. She should have called first.

When Mildred ushered them into the kitchen for cake, they fell into a conversation about Angel and Hunter's trip to Oklahoma. It seemed to take Evelyn's mind off her troubles, and for that Angel was thankful. By the time she stood to leave, Evelyn seemed more like her normal self. She hoped Hunter saw that when he came home and would relax enough to call her and talk for a while. Finding time to be together was going to be tricky, but just hearing his voice would make her days brighter. They'd figure things out because she no longer doubted that she loved him, and she hoped their night together was evidence that he loved her, as well.

Mildred stepped out onto the porch with her. "Thanks for coming by. I can see a big difference in her since you got here."

"I'm happy to help. I wish I could do more."

Mildred directed her attention out toward the pasture but didn't say anything.

"What is it?"

Mildred shook her head. "I don't understand God's mysterious ways sometimes. Why do good families have to suffer so much while vile people get to live in luxury?"

"I don't know. As I told Julia, life just isn't fair."

"That's the truth. That boy has been like a second son to me, and it's breaking my heart to see him so worried about his mother. I'm afraid the financial strain is going to break him." She gestured toward the pasture. "He's gone to see about selling off the herd and may sell the pastureland so he can afford in-home care for Evelyn while he works."

"If he sells the ranch, what will he do?"

"If I know that boy, as much as he can. If he could work twenty-four/seven, he would."

As Angel drove home, her heart weighed heavy in her chest. She wished there was some way she could magically make Hunter's life easier. She'd do anything to keep him from working himself into an early grave and leaving her to mourn the man who meant more to her than she'd ever thought possible. The man who had reopened her heart.

Angel spent the rest of the day burying herself in work. She weeded the garden, finished printing and matting several photos to be shipped out to customers, and helped Julia work on her family tree project. Julia had decided to do double the work, creating a tree for the family she'd known her entire life and one that included Nora and the family ties they were both just now beginning to explore.

Needing to stretch her legs after sitting at the kitchen table with Julia for a couple of hours, she walked down the driveway to the mailbox. Light was fading in the west and her thoughts drifted back to Hunter. She wondered if he'd found any buyers for his herd. Her heart ached at the thought of his having to sell off a big part of his own heritage in order to take care of his mother. She wondered how Evelyn would react when she found out, because Mildred had said Hunter hadn't told his mother what he was going to do. No doubt she'd feel guilty even though it wasn't her fault. No one chose to get Alzheimer's disease.

When she reached the mailbox, she pulled out the stack of flyers and envelopes. As she started back toward the house, she flipped through that day's postal offerings. She stopped in her tracks and her breath caught when she saw the envelope from *West* magazine. Her heart thundering, she ripped it open, giving herself a paper cut in the process. She cursed but didn't slow down. She unfolded the single sheet of paper inside and speed-read it. Then she went back and read it again, afraid she'd not seen the words correctly the first time.

Nope, they were still the same. She squealed and did a spirited happy dance in the middle of the driveway. Then she ran all the way back to the house and nearly burst through the door without opening it first.

"What's wrong?" her mom asked as she hurried into the living room from the kitchen.

Angel waved the letter in the air. "*West* magazine is going to print some of my photos, an entire feature. Mom, they're going to use one on the cover!"

After Angel, her mom and Julia did another excited dance in the living room, Angel knew she had to call Hunter. She hoped it wasn't insensitive to share her happy news when he was facing such an uphill battle in his own life, but he'd been so supportive. And other than her family, he meant more to her than anyone in the world.

Wanting some privacy, she headed back outside and walked past the barn until she reached the gate that led into the pasture. She pulled out her phone and dialed Hunter's number. Unable to stand still, she paced as it rang and rang and rang again. She expected the voice mail to cue her to leave a message just as Hunter said, "Hello."

"Hey, how are you?"

"Tired." He paused, and it was the kind of pause that caused a little ball of dread to form in Angel's stomach. "I heard you came by today. Sorry I wasn't here."

"It's okay. I should have called, but I had a nice time with your mom and Mildred."

He didn't respond, but she heard the closing of a door in the background and then what sounded like a breeze. Maybe he'd stepped outside for some privacy, as well.

"I'm calling with some good news. *West* magazine is going to feature some of my photos. And they're giving me the cover."

"That's great. But they're not *giving* you the cover. You earned it."

She smiled despite the fact that the distance in his voice didn't match the supportive words.

"That's sweet of you to say. I was hoping maybe we could do something to celebrate. I know you can't leave your mom, but I thought—"

"Angel."

She did not like the way he said her name, and that dread inside her ballooned in size.

"I hate to do this, but I can't be in a relationship right now. It wouldn't be fair to you."

Everything in her screamed, "No!"

"Hunter, I understand you don't have much free time."

"I don't have *any*. As in not one minute. My mom told me I should put her in the nursing home, and it damn near broke my heart. Not only will I not do that just to make my life easier, but I couldn't afford it anyway." He took what sounded like a shaky breath as tears pooled in her eyes, distorting her view of the darkening world around her. "I knew this was coming, told myself I shouldn't get involved with you, but I was selfish. I'm truly sorry about that."

"Hunter—"

"I don't have anything to give you, Angel, and you deserve so much. You and Julia."

"We can find a way to make this work," she said. "True, it won't be easy, but you know what they say about things worth having."

"You have no idea how much I want that to be true. And believe me, I've run it over and over and over in my head until I'm sure I've formed ruts through my brain. But right now, at least, I just can't see how to make it work. I have no idea how Mom's disease is going to progress, at what pace, but she has to be my main focus. There's no one else. And, Angel, I know you say we can make it work, but you deserve more than an occasional few minutes I might be able to scrape together."

"I could help."

Though she couldn't see him, she imagined him shaking his head. There was something in the air that caused that picture to form.

"Your time should go to your career, to Julia, your family. And it hurts to think about Julia getting closer to my mom only to watch her gradually forget her."

Angel understood everything he was saying, maybe even agreed with some of it, but it hurt nonetheless. She wanted to say she had enough love to sustain them both no matter what came their way, but she swallowed the words. She'd thought that once before, but it hadn't been true then. And it wasn't true now. Yes, she loved Hunter, but he evidently couldn't meet her halfway. He might not be leaving Blue Falls so fast he left scorch marks behind, but he was leaving her just the same.

He said something else, but her ears were roaring so much that she couldn't make out the words. The next thing she heard was the dial tone. Feeling as if she'd been taken to the peak of the highest mountain only to be tossed off, she sank to the ground and let the sudden, all-consuming grief overtake her. She'd allowed herself to love again, even more deeply this time, only to be abandoned once again. It wasn't the same circumstances, of course, but that didn't make the pain ripping her apart from the inside out any less excruciating.

Chapter 14

"So, how are you doing?" Chris asked Angel as they walked side by side along the edge of the pasture.

"Fine."

"Uh-huh," he said, not sounding the least bit convinced.

It didn't take a genius to figure out that the past two weeks had been some of the loneliest of her life. It was why she'd invited Chris over for a horseback ride, hoping it would take her mind off the distinct lack of Hunter in her life.

"No sense in wallowing because I can't change things."

"I hate to see you give up so easily when you still have a chance."

Angel heard the layer of sorrow in his voice. He didn't have the option of finding another path to being with the person he loved. She reached out and took his hand.

"I should be asking you how you're doing."

He shrugged as he looked out into the distance. "Some good moments peppered in between some not-so-good ones."

"Have you talked to your parents?"

"Some, but it's still really tense. I've lost count how many times I've second-guessed coming home."

She wrapped her arm around his and steered him back in the direction of the house, surprised to see how far they'd walked. "Well, you're always welcome here, you know that."

He smiled. "You're a good friend. That's why I want to see you happy."

She sighed. "Trust me, I've tried to figure out a way, but while Hunter's mom is still alive I don't see how. And I would never wish her ill. She's a good person, like he is." She looked up at the wide blue sky, which didn't match her mood lately. "Some things just aren't meant to be."

They walked in silence as she wished that Chris had Darren back and some miracle would happen and she could be with Hunter. She couldn't even hate him, not when his reason for not being with her had everything to do with the kind, selfless, hardworking son he was to his mother. He wouldn't be the same person she'd fallen in love with if he could just stick his mom in a home so he could be free of responsibility. As much as she hurt and as much as a part of her might always feel easily abandoned, she couldn't say she wouldn't have done the same thing in his situation.

She counted her blessings that her parents were still healthy and that she had plenty of family to share the work if they did eventually fall ill. She couldn't imagine being as alone as Hunter was, how the early death of his father had likely turned him into the type of person who felt he had to shoulder all the burden himself and not bother others.

"But maybe some things are," Chris said.

"Huh?"

"Despite what I've been through, I believe if people are meant to be together, they will be. And you and Hunter are meant to be together."

His belief was still echoing in her head as she watched him drive away. Part of her was ashamed that she was so wrapped up in her own loneliness when she was surrounded by people who loved her. Chris was so much more alone. Despite having his mother, Hunter was more alone. Nora was alone.

The thought of her birth mother and how they'd been getting to know each other better via phone calls and emailed photos gave her an idea. What if…?

She hurried inside, her thoughts traveling at light speed.

"Did you two have a nice ride?" her mom asked when Angel walked into the kitchen. There was no mistaking the question, perhaps even disapproval, in her mother's voice.

Angel sank into the chair opposite where her mom was clipping coupons. "I'm going to tell you something but you cannot tell a soul, not even Dad. It's not really my secret to tell, but I don't want you worrying about something where there's nothing to worry about."

"Okay," her mom said as she placed her scissors down.

"There's nothing between me and Chris but friendship. He's gay."

Her mom's eyes widened a bit before she leaned back in her chair. "That poor boy."

"What?" Surely her mom—

"No, no, that's now what I meant," her mom said with a shake of her head. "I just know how difficult that must be with his parents, his mother especially. She's not what I'd call open-minded. Or even motherly, if I'm being honest. Now it makes total sense why he left town as soon as he could."

"And why he didn't want to date me."

"Also that. Why did he come back?"

"Trying to mend fences." Angel wasn't going to share any more of Chris's story. It was up to him when and with whom to share those details.

"I hope it works out for him."

"Me, too. And speaking of things working out, I just had an idea and I need you to tell me whether it's crazy."

"This have to do with Hunter?"

"How did you know?"

"Because you're head over heels in love with him and have been miserable ever since the two of you broke up."

Angel acknowledged the truth of her mom's assessment before outlining her brainstorm. When she was finished, she held her breath and didn't release it until she saw her mother smile.

"You don't need my blessing, if that's what you're looking for, but you've got it." Her mom reached across the table and wrapped Angel's hands in hers. "I like this plan, and if it works how you hope it will, don't let Hunter say no. I admire that boy so much for what he's doing, but I want him to be happy. And you, my dear, are what makes him happy."

"I hope you're right."

"I am."

With hope welling up inside her, Angel headed outside to make a very important phone call. One that had the potential to be life changing.

Hunter didn't think he'd ever been so tired in his entire life. Not even in the days after his father's death had fatigue weighed him down so much. Add to that the fact of how hollow he was inside and that his mother was angry at him, and he felt about three seconds away from collapse all the damn time. But he didn't have time to collapse.

While Mildred and his mom's other friends stayed with her, only adding to her frustration and irritation and making her feel like a child or an invalid, he worked from before sunrise until late at night. In addition to keeping the ranch running until he could find a buyer for the herd and the rangeland who'd be willing to let him keep the acreage that held the house, he was also working roofing jobs, had a couple of shifts a week making deliveries for the lumber company and was even delivering pizzas for Gia's one night a week.

Desperate to bring in money any way he could, he'd even taken a few of his little carved horses to a gift shop in Fredericksburg, too embarrassed to try in Blue Falls in case he was rejected. To his complete surprise, the shop owner had loved the horses and said she'd take whatever he had for a commission on each sale. Now he spent every free moment on lunch breaks or right before he went to bed at night carving more.

If only he could find a way to stay awake longer, but he knew he had to sleep. He didn't tell anyone about falling asleep at the wheel the night before on his way home, waking up as he crossed the center line when the driver of an oncoming car honked at him.

But he had to make money and fast. He couldn't depend on his mom's friends staying with her all the time. They had lives to lead and as his mom's condition worsened, he didn't want to expose anyone other than himself or a paid professional caregiver to the potential hazards and heartbreak. But those caregivers didn't come cheap.

An image of Angel came to him, and his heart felt as if it was going to literally break. She'd been the one truly wonderful thing in his life, and he'd had to let her go.

You chose to, a voice in his head whispered.

But with what lay ahead, it wouldn't be fair to her. He remembered Mildred's warning about not setting himself up as some sort of martyr. That wasn't his intent. He was just a guy trying to do right by everyone he cared about. Lord knew he'd beg Angel to forgive him and take him back if he could figure out how to make a living, take care of his mom and give Angel and Julia the safe, secure, happy lives they deserved. But no matter how hard he tried, he couldn't find a way to do it all.

He couldn't be a good romantic partner, not when he was mentally and physically spent all the time. And after what had happened with Julia, he couldn't guarantee their safety. Not to mention as he'd told Angel, it would be cruel to allow Julia to become attached to his mom only to see her deteriorate. Sure, his mom might have several mostly fine years left, but there was no putting the brakes on Alzheimer's disease or reversing the damned disease. At least not yet.

He stopped at the mailbox to grab a bunch of sales flyers for things he couldn't afford, tossed them onto the seat beside him and headed up the driveway toward the house. His heart rate kicked up several notches when he spotted a familiar vehicle. As he drew close, he saw Angel sitting on the lowered tailgate of her truck. Damn, it was good to see her, but it made his heart ache at the same time because nothing had changed.

When he parked and cut off the engine, he didn't immediately get out of his own truck. He was so tired he had no doubt that he could fall asleep where he sat. And he didn't know how he was going to face Angel knowing that he still hadn't been able to find some miraculous way to give her the life he wanted to.

Somehow he found the strength to get out and face her.

"You look worn-out," she said by way of greeting.

"That's because I am."

She patted the tailgate beside her. Despite how part of him feared to get too close to her, he sank onto the spot she'd indicated.

"How have you been?" he asked.

"Busy."

"I know the feeling."

"And missing you."

He closed his eyes and barely resisted rubbing against the ache in his chest. "I know that one, too."

"What if I told you that we didn't have to miss each other anymore?"

His heart feeling as if it weighed a ton, threatening to crush him, he turned slightly toward her. "Angel, I want that more than anything, but nothing's changed."

She smiled. "That's where you're wrong."

Confusion twisted around the fatigue in his brain. "What do you mean?"

"I've found you some help."

"I can't afford it yet."

She wrapped her hand around his. "You don't have to."

"I don't understand."

"You remember how Nora said she worked in a nursing home and had experience with dementia patients?"

He nodded.

"Well, we've been talking, and she wants to get to know me and Julia better. She said nothing is keeping her in Oklahoma, so she's moving here."

"That's great. I'm happy for you."

He still wasn't connecting all the dots.

"She's going to be working part-time at the nursing home here, but she can help take care of your mom."

He was already shaking his head.

"Just stop," Angel said, gripping both of his hands now. "She wants to make a deal with you. She's sold her house and bought a small RV. If she can hook it up here, she wouldn't have to pay for a space in a campground or buy land of her own."

"That seems way too little payment for being a caretaker."

"That wouldn't be the only payment. She wants to do this for me because she wants me to be happy. And you, Hunter Millbrook, make me happy."

He just stared at this beautiful, amazing woman, not trusting that this wasn't all just a dream.

"You don't hate me?"

Now she was the one to look confused. "Why would I hate you?"

"Because I left you." He swallowed against a sudden, uncomfortable lump in his throat. "I knew how you felt about being left, and I did it anyway." He hadn't known how to avoid it without condemning her to a relationship in which he'd largely be missing, but he hated how much he may have hurt her anyway.

"I won't lie and say it didn't break my heart. But while part of me was angry, another part understood. You were in a position I wouldn't wish on anyone."

He lifted a hand and caressed her cheek. "I'm so sorry. The last thing in the world I ever wanted to do was hurt you."

"I know," she said. "But that can be behind us now if you'll agree to this plan."

Though he'd been carrying all the responsibility on his shoulders for what seemed like forever, he found himself nodding. He didn't think he had the strength to deny himself any longer. Still...

"I'll have to ask Mom. I honestly don't know if she'll go for it." To be this close to a possible solution and not be able to take it might break him.

"She's agreed."

That surprised him. "You talked to her already."

"I wanted to make sure she would be okay with it before I got your hopes up. If she wasn't, I'd decided not to upset you anymore."

He just stared at Angel, marveling at this woman who'd stolen his heart. No, not stolen. He was giving it to her freely.

"What about Julia?"

Angel smiled and nodded at the house. "She's in there with your mom and Mildred. We had a long talk about what was likely to come in the years ahead. It makes her sad, but she also understands. She loves your mom."

If this was all a dream, he hoped he never woke up.

"My God, I love you." He pulled her into his arms and

kissed her with all the bottled-up emotion he'd been carrying around inside him since the last time he'd seen her.

When they finally came up for air, her eyes were bright with unshed tears. "Do you mean it? Because I don't think I can stand to lose you again."

He framed her face with his hands. "Yes, I love you, with all my heart. I felt like I died inside when I pushed you away. I felt like the worst person on the planet and didn't know how to make everything right. But I'll make it right now. I will never, ever leave you again."

A couple of tears escaped her eyes as she looked up at him. "After Dave left, I didn't think I could ever allow myself to love someone again. It felt too dangerous. But I was wrong. I love you, too, Hunter Millbrook."

And then she slipped off the tailgate, lifted onto her toes and kissed him with so much emotion that it nearly knocked him over. Wait, something actually did run into him. Angel must have felt it, too, because she broke the kiss and looked down at the same time he did. There, hugging their legs and looking up at them with a huge smile and big, dark eyes was Julia.

"Are you going to get married?" she asked.

"Julia," Angel said, evidently embarrassed.

Hunter smiled as he rubbed his hand over Julia's silky hair. His gaze met Angel's.

"Maybe someday. I'd be one lucky man."

"Does that mean Evelyn would be my grandma, too?"

Angel rolled her eyes, but Hunter looked down at Julia's hopeful expression. His heart opened even more and he knew he'd do whatever he could to protect this precious little girl as well as her mother.

"Yes," he said as he glanced toward the porch to find his mom and Mildred standing there, both with wide smiles threatening to take over their faces. "And I know she'd love that."

"Darn right, I would," his mom called out.

Julia released them and jumped up and down. "Yes! Three grandmas! Awesome!"

Hunter and Angel laughed, but as Julia ran back toward the porch and no doubt some spoiling by the two women there, Hunter pulled Angel close.

"I wish I had the right words to tell you just how happy I am right now."

"You could always show me."

He lowered his lips to hers and did exactly that.

* * * * *

"You kissed me," he reminded her.

"The first time," she acknowledged.

"You kissed me back the second time."

"Has any woman ever not kissed you back?" she wondered.

"I'm not interested in any other woman right now," he told her. "I'm only interested in you."

The intensity of his gaze made her belly flutter. "I've got three kids," she reminded him.

"That's not what's been holding me back."

"What's holding you back?"

"I'm trying to respect our working relationship."

"Yeah, that complicates things," she agreed. Then she finished the wine in her glass and pushed away from the table. "Will you excuse me for a minute? I just want to give my mom a call to check on the kids."

"Of course," he agreed. "But I can't promise the rest of that tart will be there when you get back."

She gave one last, lingering glance at the pastry before she said, "You can finish the tart."

He was tempted by the dessert, but he managed to resist. He didn't know how much longer he could hold out against his attraction to Macy—or if she wanted him to.

Had he crossed a line by flirting with her? She hadn't reacted in a way that suggested she was upset or offended, but she hadn't exactly flirted back, either.

"Is everything okay?" he asked when she returned to the table several minutes later.

She nodded. "I got caught in the middle of an argument."

"With your mom?"

"With myself."

His brows lifted. "Did you win?"

"I hope so," she said.

Then she set an antique key on the table and slid it toward him.

Don't miss
Claiming the Cowboy's Heart *by Brenda Harlen,*
available February 2019 wherever
Harlequin® Special Edition *books and ebooks are sold.*

www.Harlequin.com

Need an adrenaline rush from nail-biting tales
(and irresistible males)?

Check out **Harlequin Intrigue®**
and **Harlequin® Romantic Suspense** books!

New books available every month!

CONNECT WITH US AT:

Facebook.com/groups/HarlequinConnection

Facebook.com/HarlequinBooks

Twitter.com/HarlequinBooks

Instagram.com/HarlequinBooks

Pinterest.com/HarlequinBooks

ReaderService.com

**ROMANCE WHEN
YOU NEED IT**

SGENRE2018

Love Harlequin romance?

DISCOVER.

Be the first to find out about promotions,
news and exclusive content!

Facebook.com/HarlequinBooks

Twitter.com/HarlequinBooks

Instagram.com/HarlequinBooks

Pinterest.com/HarlequinBooks

ReaderService.com

EXPLORE.

Sign up for the Harlequin e-newsletter and
download a free book from any series at
TryHarlequin.com.

CONNECT.

Join our Harlequin community to share
your thoughts and connect with other
romance readers!
Facebook.com/groups/HarlequinConnection

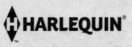

HARLEQUIN®

**ROMANCE WHEN
YOU NEED IT**

HSOCIAL2018